Auditing
Can Be Deadly

Ron Day

© Copyright Ron Day, Australia 2021

Morris Publishing Australia

http://morrispublishingaustralia.com

NATIONAL
LIBRARY
OF AUSTRALIA

A catalogue record for this
work is available from the
National Library of Australia

Auditing
Can Be Deadly

ISBN: 978-0-6452388-5-3

The right of Ron Day to be identified as the author of this work has been asserted by him.

Contents

Dedication

Dedicated to my lovely wife, Elaine, who supports my writing endeavours with a smile and words of praise.

I would like also to dedicate this, the first in a series of murder mysteries, to those who delight in reading these mysteries and who try to guess the perpetrator before the climactic scene.

Chapter 1

I bent down to tie a loose shoelace.

Clang! Clang!

A heavy throwing knife hit the concrete wall of the football stadium corridor and fell to the floor beside me. I had bent down just in time.

Surprise mingled with fear then morphed into anger. *'Who? Why?'*

My Irish was now really up. My tiger rose from the dark recesses of my mind. It reared and snarled, magnifying my anger. I scrambled to my feet; the shoelace tied in a quick knot.

'Don't touch the knife,' my companion shouted.

He bent down and carefully placed it inside an evidence bag. My eyes popped.

'Do you carry those things with you everywhere you go?'

'All the time.'

Ken never ceased to amaze me. He was a Detective Inspector, and we were football buddies, when he could get time off work to attend a match.

I looked around. A figure pushed against the tide of blue and yellow-jacketed supporters flooding into the stadium, storm water streaming from their hats and hoods.

'There he goes,' I shouted. 'Come on.'

I ran after the fleeing figure. Ken followed close behind, shoving the packaged knife into his coat pocket as he ran.

A thunderous roar from the crowd echoed from wall to wall along the concrete walkways as we raced down the wide staircase. The umpire had bounced the ball to begin the game. The stirring applause for the home team lent wings to our feet as we jumped down two stairs at a time. We would miss this important match, but attempted murder took precedence, especially when I was the intended victim.

Ahead we saw the figure racing to an entrance. He shoved the guard to one side and scrambled around bollards and tapes.

'Stop that man,' I called as I ran towards the guard.

He restrained me as I attempted to use the same exit. 'What's going on?'

Ken flashed his ID card and shouted, 'That bloke tried to knife my mate. Let us through. Quick.'

The guard threw down the barrier to give us a clear path.

We ran into the blustering storm. Rain drenched us but we doggedly followed the dark blur as it raced between parked cars and headed for the road.

As we broke clear of the park and reached the footpath, we saw the figure jump into a waiting car.

'Get the number,' shouted Ken.

I ran onto the road to read the registration number as the vehicle sped away.

'284 MVZ.'

Ken pulled out his phone, called his base and identified himself. 'Get me the owner of this car,' he barked and supplied the registration number.

The response came back almost immediately. Ken's face fell. His voice betrayed his frustration.

'Bugger! When it is found, I want it thoroughly finger-printed,' he ordered.

'Stolen this morning,' he said to me. 'We can't identify the guy from that right now. Perhaps the fingerprints on the knife will give us some answers. We'll take it straight in.'

Rain streamed off us as Ken and I jogged to his car. He opened the doors and slapped a magnetic flashing light on the roof. We took off as if the Hound of the Baskervilles was after us.

'Who was the goon who tried to knife me?' I mused as we shot down the road towards police headquarters. 'I'd like to meet him with an iron bar in my hand.'

'Make sure he has a weapon and makes the first move,' advised Ken sensibly. 'Then you are just protecting yourself.'

I imagined my fanciful thinking was no more than sheer bluff, but later I was to remember this thought.

Cars moved sideways to let us through busy intersections as Ken held his hand on the horn to reinforce our urgent need to pass.

We pulled up outside police headquarters in record time.

'Come on,' said Ken, 'Follow me.'

He sprinted to the entrance, his lean and fit body making easy work of it. I followed as quickly as my under-exercised legs would allow. I quickly felt the pain caused by too many hours spent on an office chair in front of a computer. I made a mental note to build regular exercise into my too sedentary life.

We dashed up the stairs to the forensic lab. The tech checked the knife and then searched his computer database.

He eventually came back to us.

'We have some prints on the knife but no record of anybody with those prints in our database. Sorry.'

I wonder if we'll ever find him, I thought.

'Keep them on record. We may find a match later,' Ken said to the tech. Then he turned to me. 'Come on. I'll buy you a stiff Scotch and you can tell me why someone wants you dead.'

'Make that a stiff Irish. Nothing beats an aged Jameson.'

Ken smiled. 'OK, a stiff Irish whiskey.'

Was this attempt on my life linked to my current work? Only time would tell, I mused as we travelled to the nearest pub.

* * *

A week earlier my mobile phone had grabbed my attention with its shrill buzz.

Who can that be? I asked myself, not expecting a call.

'Sean speaking,' I answered.

'Meet me for lunch. I have a problem that you may be able to help me with.'

It was David Armstrong, an old friend from university days. He was now CEO of *New Age Winery*.

After a quick lunch we sat looking at each other. Stress tightened his face and ironed out his normal smile. His red and puckered eyes betrayed a lack of sleep. He was not his usual ebullient self. The smart business suit did nothing to hide his state of panic. I guessed his job was on the line.

'What's the matter, David?' I asked with concern.

'I'm worried about the operation of the winery,' he began. 'Profits are down, and the shareholders are getting jumpy. The operation seems to be running smoothly but something is not right.'

'How can I help?'

'I would like you to cast your eyes over the winery operations. I've looked at reports from every aspect of the business, but I can't spot anything out of the ordinary.'

'Sounds like the challenge I need right now.'

My forensic accountancy service and IT work had been pedestrian lately and I needed a new challenge. I thrived on seeking the solution to puzzles and David's offer came just at the right time.

'Good,' said David. 'I'm giving you carte blanche to audit every aspect of the business.'

'Including the quality of the wine?' I asked. That would be an enjoyable bonus.

David laughed. 'Yes. I remember you like a splash or two of the red stuff. But after work mind you!'

'That's fine, David. Perhaps you can give me a guided tour of the best vintages.'

My taste buds warmed to the approaching opportunity and a smile spread across my face. It sounded like a dream. A chance to delve into the workings of a winery to identify why money was disappearing provided a challenge I would enjoy; and working with my old friend would be a bonus.

But if I'd known what was to come, I might have asked him to find another auditor.

Chapter 2

The next day, I drove up Magill Road and took the winding narrow road that climbs to Lenswood in the Adelaide Hills where the winery is situated.

As I travelled, I admired the kaleidoscopic autumn colours decorating farms and framing country cottages. Above me an azure sky spread a welcome to the morning. I smiled. I loved these mornings. The chilly air brought frost to the grass and thick fog to the deep gullies.

Watch the road, Sean, I told myself. *This one is treacherous.*

The road had been carved from the side of a steep cliff. Above the road, the cliff face rose straight up, almost to the clouds. On the other side of the road, it dropped hundreds of metres into deep valleys. It was not uncommon for a car to leave the road and tumble down the steep slopes. It was a dangerous stretch of country road and needed an alert mind, steady hands on the wheel and a light foot on the accelerator. With my heart in my mouth, I held the steering wheel tightly and fixed my eyes on the next bend.

As I stepped from the car, I heard the raucous laughing of kookaburras in the nearby eucalyptus trees. I smiled at their hilarious rising chortling call. I loved the sound. It was so unmistakably Australian, a real icon of the bush.

I approached the sprawling winery buildings and was almost overwhelmed by the sweet, musty smell of fermenting grapes. *It's definitely a winery,* my appreciative nose told me.

An attractive woman hovered near the administration entrance awaiting my arrival. She was dressed in a smart suit that fitted her like a glove. Her blue eyes smiled warmly as she shook my hand with a firm grip.

'Good morning. You must be Sean. My name is Angela,' she said.

'Good morning, Angela,' I replied with what I hoped was an engaging smile. 'I didn't expect to find an angel here now,' I said with a touch of my native Irish brogue. I hadn't kissed the Blarney Stone for nothing.

She smiled. 'The CEO and senior executives are waiting for you in the Boardroom.'

She indicated the direction to the room politely with a quick sideways movement of her head that made her golden locks dance a sinuous tango around her shoulders. I realised I was still holding her hand. She glanced down so I let it go reluctantly and followed her. She turned and led me down a long corridor. Our footsteps echoed on the polished wooden floors as we headed for the boardroom. The walls were festooned with awards. Most were from Australian wine competitions, but several were from European countries.

David was CEO of a successful winery with an impressive record.

David must employ some top winemakers, I thought.

The Boardroom was in keeping with the rest of the building. David sat at the head of a long oak table that dominated the room. My eyes swiftly assessed the well-dressed men and women seated around the table. I could see no hint of a welcoming smile on any of those professional faces. A secretary sat to one side, her fingers dancing across her computer keyboard.

David rose as I entered the room and reached to shake my hand.

'Welcome, Sean. So glad you could make the meeting this morning. Please take a seat near me and I'll introduce you to the team.'

'As I mentioned previously,' he turned to the executives, 'I have been requested by the Board to employ an auditor to check our business processes and accounts. Like me, the Board members are concerned with the drop in profits over the last six months or more and have requested an independent review. Sean O'Connor is a qualified auditor, forensic accountant, and IT specialist. I recommend him to you.'

He named each member of the executive team around the table and gave a short description of their roles.

I looked around the table. A sea of stony faces greeted me.

Ouch! I thought. *What have I got myself into?*

The air pulsed with negativity and distrust – and something more. This was clearly an unwanted intrusion.

Some of the eyes viewed me speculatively. Unvoiced hostility jostled active hate for ascendancy on some faces.

Oh well, I thought. *They'll just have to accept it. Every business needs a regular audit.*

'Would you like to tell the group how you will proceed, Sean?' asked David.

I stood and addressed the group quietly but insistently. 'I realise audits are an intrusion, but I will try to minimise interruptions to your routine. However, I will have questions from time to time for each of you. I will look at every aspect of the business from winemaking, through bottling and warehousing to sales, marketing, and distribution. I will investigate the purchasing processes, the accounting, HR, and payroll. At the end of my audit, I will prepare a full report. I'll conclude with an address to this group. Are there any questions?'

The silence was deafening.

'Thank you, Sean,' David rescued the moment. 'When can you start?'

'Next Monday, if that suits you,' I replied.

'That will be fine. Angela will take you on a tour of the site and show you where to find the resources you need. I have sent a message to every team leader to give you full cooperation.'

Angela rose from her seat, and I stood and followed her to the door.

'They're a cheerful bunch,' I remarked as we returned to the corridor. 'I didn't win too many friends.'

'They're OK,' she replied, 'but no one likes audits. They'll get used to you being around in a day or two. I'm glad you're here,' she added.

'Does that mean you'll have dinner with me?' I responded cheekily.

'We'll see.'

I took a quick glance and saw the trace of a grin on her lips.

Promising start, I thought.

'Let me take you on a quick tour so you get the feel of the place.'

* * *

Harvest was in full swing, and people ran to and fro. Some directed trucks as they offloaded grapes into the crushers; others supervised the processes of removing leaves and twigs before pumping the grapes to fermenters. Pumps pulsated, voices echoed around the cavernous building, bottles rattled on the bottling line. The smell of fermenting grapes laced the air. Forklifts danced around obstacles as they loaded and offloaded pallets of chemicals and packaged wine.

Apprentice winemakers tested baumé and acid levels and recorded pH readings meticulously. Acid and yeast were added in carefully measured quantities. Winemakers are skilled chemists who manipulate chemicals, temperatures, and the use of oak to achieve appropriate results for the different grape varieties.

As we walked, Angela introduced me to some of the staff. The one I liked most on first meeting was the Chief Winemaker, Tony Antenucci. He was a tall man with a proud bearing.

I soon discovered he set exacting standards for his staff, could be cuttingly cruel when someone made what he considered a stupid mistake but balanced that by praising good practice.

'How much do you know about winemaking?' he asked.

'Enough to know I should leave it to experts like you.'

'Good. Then we'll get along fine. Just don't get under my feet when things are busy. What information do you need from me?'

I pondered for a moment. 'Who on your team do you trust least?'

'Direct, aren't you? I like that. If I was to give everyone in my team a score out of ten for honesty, there are two people I would give a minus score.'

'And they are?'

He gave me the names and I made notes.

'Thank you, Tony,' I said as Angela re-appeared to take me back to the car park.

Chapter 3

The Monday following the football match I began my auditing.

Angela met me in the foyer. 'Where would you like to start?' she asked.

I smiled warmly at her. I was forming a strong bond with this beautiful woman. I loved the way she looked. I loved the way she got to the point with no airs and graces.

'Can we begin with Tony in the winemaking area?'

I could tell she liked my positive approach.

'Let's go,' she said. She turned and began walking down the corridor away from the foyer.

We dodged forklift trucks and pumps and stepped over thick hoses as we made for the raised platform in the centre of the winemaking area. We could see Tony pointing something out to a worker from his raised position.

We approached him just as he finished his conversation.

'Good morning, Tony. Do you have the time to give me a quick introduction to your area in the winery?' I called politely.

'Sure. Come up here for a moment, you two,' he said indicating the stairs.

We climbed to the platform and gazed down into a huge fermentation tank. Deep red bubbles burped as fruit sugars and yeast matured into alcohol. A pump flushed the floating grapes on the top of the tank with liquid taken from the bottom to get colour from the skins.

'From here you can see the extent of my domain.'

As he talked, he waved his arms to indicate the forest of fermentation tanks, pumps, ladders and gantries, and the lab where chemists carried out wine analysis.

A shadow crossed the surface of the wine before us.

'Look out,' called Tony. He grabbed our shoulders and pulled us back.

A heavy 20 litre metal keg brushed my arm before hitting the platform with a loud thump and rolling into the bubbling wine. As it hit the surface it sprayed dull red wine droplets over us. Our clothes looked like they had developed measles.

This was too much of a coincidence. My inner tiger leapt forward and swung his head looking for other danger. *A knife was thrown at me at the football and now a heavy metal keg threatened to knock my brains out. What was going on?*

I stood glued to the floor, stunned. My body refused to move. This was too much. *What have I done? Why am I the target*?

Then I looked at Angela. Her shoulders were bunched, and tears streamed down her face. She held her hands to her mouth as if to stifle a scream. She had been badly frightened by the incident. I pulled her into a tight hug and held her until her tears stopped and her body relaxed.

'Shhhh!' I said, 'Shhhh!' like a parent quietening a frightened child.

She slowly relaxed and I loosened my grip.

'Was that an accident?' Her tiny voice betrayed her fear.

'I don't think so,' I replied. 'That is probably the second time someone has tried to kill me.'

'The second?' She shuddered. Her mouth and eyes opened wide.

'Someone threw a knife at me at the football on Saturday.'

'What's going on?' she asked. She grabbed me tightly.

'There's something happening here at the winery that someone doesn't want me to find.'

'Be careful, Sean. I don't want you dead,' she whispered and hugged me with an intensity I hadn't expected.

I hugged her back with an equal intensity, delighting in the feel of her body against mine. It took my mind off my fears and replaced them with new feelings. I cared about this woman and wanted to protect her. I wanted to be her hero. My tiger purred.

'I don't want to be dead either now I have found you,' I replied.

Steel-capped boots echoed above our heads as our presumed attacker escaped along a steel gantry that ran the length of the winery, high above our heads.

'I saw a flash of red,' I called as we attempted to pursue the runner with our eyes.

'I'll bet that was our circus performer,' said Tony. 'He always wears a red bandana.'

'Circus performer? Any chance he throws knives?' I enquired tentatively.

'Well known for it.'

'What's his job?'

'Delivery driver.'

'Any opportunity to deliver extra cases of wine to his mates?'

'Plenty.'

I pulled out my notebook.

'Is he one of the people you gave me the name off last week?'

'Yes.'

'Which one of these two names is the circus performer?'

'That one.'

He pointed to one of the names on my list. I read the name over and over. *Damian Delonga* was stamped into my mind. This was the guy I wanted to meet with an iron bar in my hand. My tiger growled his agreement.

I pointed to the other name on my list. 'What does this Steve Lucas do?'

'He's a forklift driver. Used to be a prize-fighter. Strong as an ox. Has a violent temper so most people keep out of his way.'

I added that information to my mental database for future reference.

'What's happened here?' asked a pleasant voice behind us.

'Hello, Karl,' said Tony. 'A 20-litre metal keg fell from the top gantry and only just missed us.'

'How did that happen?'

'I have no idea yet. We'll investigate later. But forgive my bad manners. Karl, this is Sean O'Connor. He's here to audit the winery. Sean, this is my right-hand man, Karl Amos. He heads the team of winemakers.'

I held out my hand to shake Karl's. 'Good to meet you,' I said.

'And you,' said Karl with a smile.

His confident manner and role in the winery for one so young spoke volumes about his ability both in his work and in his relations with other people.

'If I may interrupt, Tony,' added Karl, 'we are about to test blend a Cabernet with Merlot.' You might like to join us and give your opinion.'

'Thank you, Karl. I'll be there shortly.'

We took our leave of Tony. Angela led me back to the staff area where we could clean up. I stepped into the male bathroom and dabbed at my clothing with a damp hand towel. It was a futile effort, but I convinced myself I had made some improvement.

I joined Angela back in the staffroom where we sat nursing hot coffees.

'Can we go somewhere that has a low ceiling so objects can't fall on us?' I asked.

'Yes. I'll point out some of the offices, and then we'll go to the Sales and Marketing area.'

'Sounds good. Lead on.'

She took me on a circuitous route past the HR, Accounting and Clerical areas, describing the people who worked there and their roles.

As we passed the door of the HR department, someone stepped out in our path.

'Hello, Angela,' she said, 'Showing our guest around I see.'

'Good morning, Marie. Let me introduce you to Sean O'Connor. Sean this is Marie Young, the head of the HR department.'

'Good morning, Marie,' I said, a polite smile on my face.

'Good morning, Sean. Good luck with your auditing,' she said with a faint smile as she turned and walked briskly towards David's office.

When we reached the Sales and Marketing area I was introduced to John Cartwright, the head of this section. He was dressed in smart casual clothes and obviously took great care with his outward appearance. After a few moments of conversation, I came to the opinion that John was a born salesman with a magnetic personality that could make him your next best friend in moments. He could talk up a storm, seemingly without needing to draw breath.

Most of his staff members were busy on the phone calling clients and taking orders.

'Would you allow me to talk with some of your staff?' I asked politely when he had finished his sales pitch.

'Certainly,' John replied. 'Feel free to move around and talk with anyone you choose.'

'Thank you,' I replied and started walking among the desks.

'I'll catch up with you later,' called Angela.

I smiled my agreement.

A friendly young man looked up from his computer.

'My name is Sean. What is your name?'

'I'm Bhupinder,' he answered. His pleasant voice was soft and well-modulated.

'What is your job, Bhupinder?' I asked.

'I contact some of our regular customers and tell them about our new wines,' he replied.

'Do you have any sales figures to show me?'

'Yes,' he replied. 'I'll print you a copy of last week's figures. It was a good week.' He called up the report and sent it to a printer.

I took the report from his proffering hands and glanced down the columns. I love the way Indians offer documents and business cards with both hands. It seems to make the offer more genuine somehow. It was indeed a good week's work.

'You have done very well,' I complimented. 'You are obviously a good salesperson.'

'I like my work,' he said with a wide smile. He shook his head from side to side in that endearing way Indians use to express agreement and acknowledge praise.

'Thank you, Bhupinder,' I said.

I moved to another desk.

I spent most of the afternoon in the sales and marketing area, talking individually with each staff member, and viewing records and graphs. Everything seemed above board and most of the staff were happy in their work. They appeared to be performing well and sales were robust. I saw nothing that gave me any concern.

Angela eventually appeared so I thanked John and left with her.

'Did you find anything to worry you?' she asked.

'No. Everything seems fine.'

We walked back to the main foyer chatting about my movements for the next day. I wished her good afternoon and headed out the door to the carpark.

* * *

As I drove home that afternoon I mused over the day's events. The keg didn't drop by itself. It missed me by a whisker because of Tony's tug on my shoulder. The thought unsettled me. First there was the attempted knife murder at the football stadium and now an attempt to knock my brains out. It was too much to take in. Why did someone want me dead? What threat was I to anyone? It had to be linked to the winery.

I was as nervous as a kitten. I'd never been a threat to anyone before that I was aware of. My eyes watched the road with heightened alertness. They constantly flicked to the rear-view mirror.

Suddenly, a dark four-wheel drive vehicle raced up behind me. The hairs on the back of my neck stood to attention as my neck muscles tightened. My tiger raised his head, looked behind and snarled a deep-throated warning. Was I imagining it, or was this yet another threat? Why was it travelling so fast on this treacherous road? The cliff face on my right towered to the sky. On my left the edge of the road dropped hundreds of metres.

The dark vehicle crept closer until it was almost touching my back bumper. My nerves hit high-tension levels. This was no game. This guy was for real.

We came to a short stretch of straight road. I gasped. The following car was attempting to pass me. Was he crazy? What if another vehicle came towards us up the hill? It would cause a deadly pile up.

I felt a bump at the back of my car. No way! He was trying to run me off the road. He was trying to push me over the edge to certain death!

I planted my foot and zoomed ahead. My tiger leapt forward in full flight, willing me to go even faster. Calling on my rally driving experience, I slid around the next bend, and the next, and the next. I was gaining a little space. My low-slung front-wheel drive vehicle could corner faster than his heavier and more unstable two-tonne chariot.

My mind slipped into planning mode. I remembered that about five bends ahead was a firefighter's track up the hill and through the forest. If I could make it there, I might escape this murderous attack.

I slid around bend after bend, travelling as fast as possible. My attacker followed, dropping back a little as his vehicle lurched on the sharp bends. I knew if I waited until we reached some straighter sections of road further down the hill, I would be a dead duck.

The bush track was coming closer. As I reached it, I suddenly swung the wheel. Tyres scrabbled to hold in the soft gravel. The back of the car slid wildly but the front tyres held. *Thank God for front-wheel drive,* I thought.

I shot up the track as fast as I could. I knew it would take the other vehicle some time to stop, turn and retrace my steps. I had a small timeframe to come up with a safety strategy.

Luckily, I knew the track. A little further up this bush track was an even smaller side-track leading to a water tower where firefighters could refill the tanks on their trucks. I turned up this track and hid behind the cement tower. Soon I heard the big vehicle grinding up the hill. He missed my turn off and kept going.

I gave him a few moments to be clear before I crept out and returned to the lower road. I was never so pleased to re-join the heavy suburban traffic at the bottom of the hill.

I called Ken.

'Do you have a spare bed, Mate? I'm not game to go home tonight.'

Chapter 4

As I pulled up, Ken opened the door. 'Are you okay?' he asked.

I could tell he was genuinely concerned. He invited me into the house. 'Come and say, hello to the wife,' he said. 'She's looking forward to seeing you again.'

We walked into the kitchen, and I greeted Mandy who was mashing potatoes for our evening meal.

'Welcome, Sean,' she said.

Her open smile was a joy to see. I began to relax in its warmth. She was a regular Earth Mother type, round, warm and caring.

She wiped her hands on a towel and took mine. 'It's good to see you again. Ken has talked so much about you lately. I think he's fixated on your welfare.'

'Thank goodness he is,' I replied. 'I need a guardian angel. I couldn't go home tonight. I suspect I may have had a very unwelcome guest on the doorstep.'

'Tell us about tonight,' Ken said, 'Why are you concerned?'

I related the account of the car chase down the mountain. 'I felt certain he would visit me tonight and make another attempt on my life. I don't mind admitting

I'm feeling paranoid. Three attempts to murder me in a week are just too much to cope with.'

They both voiced their concern. I was touched by their obvious sympathy.

'Lucky you knew that firefighting track. I didn't know about that one,' added Ken.

'Back in the days when I was young and silly, I got involved in rally driving. I bought a Datsun 1600 and did all the usual things to hot it up. I polished the ports, raised the front suspension, and always carried a bag of sand in the boot to keep the back wheels on the road. Talk about a machine on steroids.

'We studied maps of the hills and the organisers devised routes along many of the little-known tracks and country roads. It was fun. Eventually I took one risk too many, rolled the car and came close to saying *Sayonara* to the world. It was time to quit.'

'I'm glad you came to your senses,' said Ken, 'Life would be dull without you around.'

'Thanks ... I think.' I pulled a sad face.

He and Mandy laughed.

We had an enjoyable meal, and I was eventually escorted to the spare bedroom. I lay on my bed, my mind churning over the events of the day. It took ages to fall asleep.

* * *

My phone danced and shrieked near my head early next morning. It woke me from a disturbing dream of cars chasing me. I jerked my body upright and almost fell from the bed in my haste to turn off the shrill alarm. But it wasn't the alarm. It was a call.

'Yes,' I mumbled.

'Get up here quickly,' shouted David.

'What? What's going on?' I struggled to gain full comprehension.

'There's a body in the big wine vat. And bring your detective mate with you.'

'OK,' I answered. I wormed my way into my clothes, fingers tangling in my haste to secure zippers and buttons.

I ran to the kitchen where Ken and Mandy were eating breakfast.

'There's a body in a wine tank,' I shouted. 'We need to get up there fast.'

'Right,' he said, 'Grab a coffee while I call up some troops.'

Mandy poured me a cup and I grabbed it with both hands. I took a big gulp, and my eyes sprang to attention.

Ken called me. I ran to his car, jumped in and we sped away, wheels screaming on a sharp corner.

As we drove into the winery car park a squad car pulled in behind us. We all hurried to the winemaking area where David waved us towards the platform overlooking the large wine vat. The fermenting wine bubbled and burped around a floating figure. The body was face down. Round his throat floated a red bandana.

What a way to go, I thought, imagining him drowning from over-drinking.

I'd seen one or two dead bodies in the past but this one left me with a sickening feeling in my stomach. On one hand, I reasoned, he was probably the one who had been trying to kill me. On the other hand, the large section of crushed bone in the back of his skull gave me goose bumps. *Someone else got to him with an iron bar before me*, I thought.

One of the uniformed policemen called for an ambulance.

'Who is this guy?' Ken asked David.

'Judging by the red bandana around his neck, I'd say it's our circus performer. His name is Damian Delonga.'

'I think this is the guy who threw a knife at me at the football,' I added. 'I wouldn't be surprised if he was also the one who threw the keg at me yesterday and tried to run me off the road last night.'

'Can you identify his vehicle?' Ken asked David.

David nodded.

'Please go with this policeman and show him the vehicle.'

'Sean. I want you to go too to see if this was the vehicle that chased you last night.'

Ken turned to the cop and said, 'When you've identified the vehicle, call for a tow truck and have it taken in for forensic analysis. I particularly want fingerprints checked to see if they are the same as the ones we found on the knife.'

I walked with David to the circus performer's car. It was a dark coloured four-wheel drive vehicle. I noted a small dent in the front left bumper where he had tried to run me off the road. I pointed that out to the policeman. He pulled out a camera and took a shot of the damage.

'Can you see that small flake of red paint?' he asked. 'Is that the colour of your car?

'Yes,' I replied. 'Well spotted.'

'It's my job,' he replied noncommittally.

'That's definitely the vehicle that tried to run me off the road last night,' I said to the policeman.

We walked back into the winery, and he repeated my observations to Ken.

Soon a siren announced the arrival of an ambulance. Two burly paramedics walked in with a stretcher. They extracted the somewhat pickled body from the wine and conveyed it to their ambulance. Before long they were on their way to the forensic pathologist's lab.

'Well,' said Ken. 'We've possibly solved one mystery. But we now have a second one. Who, I wonder, killed the would-be assassin?'

'I have part of a theory,' I replied.

'Let's hear it. Nothing is clear, so any suggestions are worth looking at.'

I started tentatively. 'It seems that this guy tried to kill me three times and failed. I'm guessing that someone was very disappointed with him and saw him as a potential threat. I'm also guessing a lot of money is involved and someone won't stop until I am out of the picture.'

'Which means,' finished Ken, 'we need to find out what is going on quickly. I'm appointing a couple of uniformed guys to watch your back every moment until this case is solved.'

I wasn't sure about having a couple of policemen tagging along but I guessed it was probably a wise idea.

'Thank you, Ken. I appreciate your concern.'

* * *

Ken called later. 'My mate at the pathology lab tells me your circus performer received a massive blow to the head. He was dead before he hit the wine.'

'So, he didn't die from drinking too much wine then,' I questioned half in jest.

'No wine in his lungs so your theory of suicide by over-imbibing doesn't hold water – or in this case wine.'

I smiled at his attempt at a joke. Ken was a facts man. He had no skills in the joking arena.

'There were possibly two people, one to hold his attention and one behind him to deliver the killing blow,' he continued.

'So, we could be looking for two people,' I summed up.

'Most likely but there could be more. A murder on top of the possible theft of a large amount of money suggests there could be a whole gang at work.'

Chapter 5

Kens' evidence gathering team arrived at the winery. David showed the group to a space he had set up as the incident room and asked Angela to help get the interviewing underway.

'Angela, we'll start with the winemakers. Who is the Chief winemaker?' Ken asked.

'Tony Antenucci,' she responded.

'Can you please ask him to come to see me?' he asked. 'We'll begin interviewing in ten minutes.'

Angela left and Ken turned to his interviewing team to instruct them on the questions to ask.

I left to continue my own investigations. My two appointed police guards followed me.

For the next three days I checked customers' invoices against delivery dockets and warehouse records. I called clients to verify that they had received the wine shown on their records. The two police officers keeping an eye on me had a boring time of it. I pointed out where they could find the staffroom and suggested they go one at a time to get a cup of coffee or something to munch on. I was quite sure one officer staring in my direction would scare off anyone planning to harm me. When I moved, they moved. Ken had given them clear instructions not to let me out of their sight. Later, when I went into David's office they stood patiently outside the door.

On close checking it became clear warehouse stock levels were dropping faster than invoiced sales indicated. After reviewing documentation for the previous three months, I determined that three or four cases of wine had been disappearing each week.

At my meeting with David that Friday afternoon I explained that the circus performer /delivery driver had been loading more wine than he needed to fill orders.

'But that is petty pilfering,' David said. 'Maybe $800 to a thousand dollars a week. That wouldn't account for the massive drop in profits.'

'Agreed,' I said, 'Something else has been happening, but at least you can now put in place some practices to stop this loss.'

'Yes. I will. I'll assign someone to check invoices against delivery dockets as the stock leaves the warehouse. Thanks, Sean. You've solved part of the problem. It seems our circus performer was making himself a few extra dollars each week selling wine to his mates.'

'But that didn't give him a reason to try to kill me. There's something else rotten in the state of Denmark,' I quoted, a line I borrowed from Shakespeare. 'And why,' I asked, 'would someone murder him? The plot thickens.'

'Let's solve it before someone else dies. It's bad for business.'

'And if it's me that dies, it's bad for my business as well,' I added drily.

'We need you too much to let that happen. Now on the brighter side, let's go and join the others at the Friday night wine tasting session. You'll enjoy that.'

'To be sure,' I said in my best Dublin accent. 'Oi'll be after enjoyin' that now I will.'

David smiled. 'You can take the boy out of the country, but you can't take the country out of the boy,' he said, borrowing a cliché that had reached its use-by-date many years ago.

I groaned.

We walked to the Board Room to find the huge oak table covered with a veritable feast of wine, plates of dry biscuits, sections of carrot and cucumber, and fruit, nuts, and other vegetables. The room was crowded with staff, family members and friends. It was a popular event.

'Where's the cheese?' I asked David. 'I thought you always had cheese with wine at these tastings.'

'No cheese, Sean,' he answered like a teacher explaining a concept to a dull student. 'Cheese coats the tongue with protein so you can't taste the finer qualities of the wine. Cheese goes with poor wine to hide the bad flavours.'

I put that in my mental memory book for the next time I went to a wine tasting.

Angela appeared with a tray of wine in tasting glasses.

'Thought you might be thirsty,' she said with a smile. 'This will wash down the dust from those old records you've been studying all week.'

I took a glass, and she explained the qualities of the Merlot she was taking around the room.

I sipped the wine and smiled. 'Just what I needed.'

Angela's face lit up in appreciation of my response before moving to the next person with her tray of wine.

One of the office staff approached me from the other side. I hadn't seen her coming.

'Here's a special wine you might like to try,' she said quietly.

I turned too swiftly, and my arm connected with her hand. The glass flew from her hand to land on the tiled floor with a crash.

'Oh,' said Angela. 'I'll get a mop,' and she hurried off.

My face fell in embarrassment. 'I'm terribly sorry,' I said to the young woman. 'I'm usually not so clumsy.'

'It's all right,' she said. 'No harm done.'

She bent down and began collecting the larger shards of glass. I bent to help and paused for a second, surprised. I could see specks of white on the pieces of glass that had formed the bowl of the glass.

I lifted one larger piece, wrapped it in my serviette and placed it in my pocket. *Am I becoming totally paranoid*? I wondered. My tiger shook his head, a snarl on his face. I wished I had one of Ken's evidence bags. I was sure that good wine didn't usually have white powder in it.

My desire to taste wine suddenly evaporated.

Angela came back with a mop, dustpan, and brush. I quickly explained what I had found and told her I was off to see Ken.

'Oh, no,' she whispered, a deeply concerned look on her face. 'Not another attempt. Isn't Ken still here?'

'No,' I replied. 'He left here some time ago. I hesitated. 'Would you have dinner with me tomorrow night?' I asked quietly. 'I would like to talk over some of the winery problems with you. It would help me clear my head on some of the issues.'

'Yes,' she replied with no hesitation. 'That is a good idea. I have some thoughts I'd like to share with you too.' Then she added, a cheeky smile on her face, 'There is one condition.'

'What's that?' I asked.

'I choose the wine.'

'What a great idea,' I said, 'I'll come for you at 7.00pm. OK?'

'Yes. That's fine.'

She dictated her address and I scribbled it on a serviette. I smiled my thanks and turned to find David. I thanked him, made my apologies, and made my way out to my car. My police escort followed closely behind and stayed the obligatory three car spaces behind all the way. It was reassuring that I wouldn't have anyone else trying to run me off the road and down the steep cliff to my death.

Before long I was knocking on Ken's door.

'Let me guess,' he said when he opened the door. 'Another crisis.'

'You could say that,' I replied. I explained the situation and took the wrapped piece of glass from my pocket.

'Don't unwrap it,' he said quickly. 'We'll get the boys in the lab to check it. Knowing your recent history, I have to take it seriously. Let's go.'

At police headquarters the lab technician carefully took the wrapped glass from me.

After a while he returned. 'I've run a few tests. I'd like to do more but there is enough evidence for me to suggest it is probably potassium cyanide. The bitter almond smell is a dead giveaway. Pardon the pun.'

I gulped. This was taking murdering me too far.

'Where would they get it from,' I asked.

'It is extracted from natural sources such as peach seeds, cherry pips and apple seeds. Small amounts won't do much damage, but large amounts can kill.

'Good thing you didn't drink the wine,' said Ken. 'Call David. See if he can identify the person who gave it to you. We need her address.'

I called David and briefly explained the problem. He was able to identify the young woman straight away.

'Give me a few moments,' he said. 'Sarah's already left but I'll get her address from my office. I'll call you back.'

Good as his word, David called back within a few minutes with Sarah's home address.

'Come on,' said Ken. 'We'll pay her a visit.'

As we pulled up outside her house, Sarah arrived home.

She climbed out of her car, and we walked over to her.

She looked up in surprise. 'Hello, Sean,' she said. 'What are you doing here?'

'Hello, Sarah,' I said. 'Detective Inspector Ken Harris has some questions for you.'

'Good evening, Sarah,' said Ken. 'This won't take very long. Can we go inside?'

'Of course,' said Sarah. She was puzzled but not evasive. She glanced quickly at the police car that had pulled up and parked in the street behind our car. We could see her face tightening with tension as she unlocked the front door and led us into the lounge room.

'I have been told you brought Sean a glass of wine that he accidentally knocked from your hand. Is that correct?'

'Yes,' she answered.

We could see she had no idea where this was going.

'Can you tell us who gave you the glass of wine for Sean?'

'Oh. Let me think. It might have been Mr Douglas. He's the Accountant.'

'Are you sure?'

'Not really. There was a lot going on and my head is a little muddled. Perhaps it was John Cartwright. He's in charge of Sales and Marketing. Or then it could have been Mrs Moore. She heads the clerical pool. Oh, I'm sorry. I just feel muddled now.'

'Don't worry, Sarah,' said Ken. 'Sleep on it tonight and call Sean if things become clearer in your head.'

'Give me your mobile phone,' I said quietly. She handed it over and I added my phone number to her contacts' list.

'Give me a call if you think of anything we need to know.'

She nodded. 'Was there something wrong with the wine?' she asked.

Ken thought a moment then answered, 'Let's say there may have been something in the glass that wasn't expected.'

'Oh! Did I do something wrong?'

'Not you, Sarah. You did nothing wrong. Just think hard about who gave you the glass.'

We made our farewells and left her home.

'Not much else we can do tonight,' said Ken as we drove back to his house. 'But I'll meet you at the winery Monday morning. I have more people to interview. We have to stop this rubbish happening.'

I drove home with my police escort following three car lengths behind. They parked in the street in front of my house. I entered and carefully locked my front door behind me. I knew another team would take over at some time during the night, so I slept soundly.

Chapter 6

I spent most of Saturday going through my notes and making a list of the questions I still needed answers for.

'Where are we going for dinner, Sean,' Angela asked when I arrived at her door that evening.

'It's a surprise.'

'No hints?'

'No hints,' I replied with a smug smile.

I started driving.

'I see your surveillance team is on duty,' she remarked as she looked through the back window to see the Police car trailing us.

'Yes. Ken's boys are looking after my welfare.'

A while later she said, 'You're pulling into Norwood Parade. It must be Italian.'

'Or Greek or Indian or Chinese or Vietnamese or ... Need I go on?'

We parked and Angela took my arm. I loved the feel of her arm wrapped around mine.

'Is it this one?' she guessed as we passed an Indian restaurant.

'Maybe,' I answered and took a pretend turn towards their door.

'Whoops. Wrong one,' I said. 'Maybe another time.'

I turned us back to the pavement.

'Don't be a tease,' she pleaded, jumping up and down in mock anger.

I smiled. When we reached my destination, I pretended to walk past then turned to the door at the very last moment.

'You're such a pain,' she said.

She waved her head from side to side to emphasise her point. Her long golden locks brushed her shoulders as they swung.

The air sizzled with Italian spices in a mouth-watering introduction to one of the Parade's most popular venues. As we walked through the door, we could see a chef spinning a circle of dough in the air, way above his head. He reached for a pizza tray and caught the doughy disk as it plunged back to earth. It settled onto its bed perfectly and customers clapped.

Waiters slid like shadows on ice as they served food and wine and collected empty plates from clients seated at a forest of tables. Noise bounced off hard surfaces and walls, tangling tones and accents from many countries into a celebration of Mediterranean cuisine.

A portly chef with his hair tucked into a tall white hat of office, opened his arms wide and made a beeline for us.

'Sean, *amico mio. Buena será.* Welcome to my humble little shop,' he boomed.

His rapid movement and loud voice opened a path through the throng. It reminded me of Moses opening a path through the Red Sea.

He grabbed me in a fierce bear hug. 'It is so long, *mio fratello*. Too, too, too long.'

Still hugging me, he swung around so he could see Angela. 'And who is this *bella donna*? It is time you found a diamond like this one.'

'Let me go, you big ape and I'll introduce you.'

'Angela, this is Marcello. He is the best restaurateur in Adelaide. Marcello, this is Angela. She is the woman I've been looking for all my life.'

'*Vieni*, come, Angela. Let me hug you too. If you are the woman who has captured Sean's heart, you are *molto benevento* – very welcome.'

Marcello let me go and gave Angela a big hug. She squirmed a little but patiently put up with being smothered by the mountain of a man.

'But I forget my manners. *Vieni*. Come.'

Before he walked away, I said, 'There are two policemen outside. I would like to buy them a pizza.'

'Police? Why?'

'I'll tell you later. It's a long story. I'll pay for this one.'

'It will be on the house,' said Marcello decisively. 'We always look after police. We want them to look after us too.'

Marcello spoke rapidly in Italian to the pizza chef then said again '*Venite, miei amici.*'

He led us through the kitchen, where we weaved our way past a heaving, shouting melee of white coated

39

chefs, flaming gas rings, saucepans, plates, bowls, and endless benches. The aromas were overpowering, and it would have been the thrill of a lifetime to taste a little of each dish being prepared. Beyond the kitchen we found a smaller discreet dining room with a single candle lit table.

'This is my treat for you. Make yourselves comfortable.'

We sat. Angela took in the wonderful atmosphere of this amazing retreat from the noise and bustle of the main dining room. Soft music played, Italian of course. This was atmosphere with a capital 'A'.

Marcello came back with two wine glasses and a special wine. Angela saw the label and her eyes popped. 'Henschke's Hill of Grace'. Marcello, we can't afford that wine. It is too expensive.'

'So, you know your wines,' he responded. 'Good.'

'But why,' she asked.

'This, bella donna, is my treat for Sean. Some years ago, we were on the rocks, I think you say. Our business was losing money and we were near to closing the doors. My house, she was, what is the word, "hocked" to the bank. They were ready to take everything. By the Grace of God, I met Sean and he saved us. Now he is my brother. He is family. When he comes, I feed him. This is what I do for family. Enjoy my treat. If you are with Sean, you are family too. Welcome to family Gambino.'

'But do we get to see a menu?' she asked.

'No bella donna. We bring food. You eat it. You get the best we can prepare.'

'This is just amazing,' she replied. 'I have never experienced such wonderful service before. I thank you very much. What do you say, *multo bene*?'

Marcello smiled broadly at her attempt to speak Italian then turned and walked back to the kitchen.

'Are you any further ahead with your investigations into the disappearing money?' asked Angela.

'Not really,' I replied, 'Although I've been able to narrow down the possibilities.'

'Who is in the clear in your mind?'

'There is nothing that I can spot in the marketing team. They are all working well, and they really have no opportunity to redirect large sums of money. Similarly, the clerical team seems to be in the clear.'

'Who does that leave?'

'Anybody in the accounting team could interfere with money transfers, but at this stage I'm putting my money on the accountant.'

'You don't like him, do you?

"He's rude, arrogant and unhelpful. No, I don't like him, and I don't trust him.'

'Are you sure he could be a thief?' Angela queried.

'No. I'm not sure, but at this stage he is definitely a suspect with means and opportunity,' I replied.

'I think we should look outside the winery. Perhaps it could be someone at the bank, or perhaps a hacker getting into our accounts,' said Angela.

'We'll look at those possibilities too,' I promised.

Our conversation was brought to a halt by the arrival of a delightfully arranged plate of antipasto. It was soon followed by a procession of delicious pasta plates.

During dinner I asked, 'Can you ride?'

She paused, her fork halfway to her mouth, her eyebrows raised in question. 'Do you own a horse?'

'Not really. It's an iron horse.'

Her surprise deepened; food forgotten. 'An iron horse?'

'Its name is Harley. It's a motor bike.'

'Oh!'

'Have you been on a bike before?'

'A couple of times.' Her face lost its look of surprise and a small smile flitted around her mouth. 'Just up and down the street on my brother's trail bike. Why do you ask?

'I'd like to take you for a ride up the freeway. Nothing dangerous. We'll have lunch in Murray Bridge overlooking the river, then take a gentle ride through the hills and back home.'

'Sounds like fun. When were you thinking of doing this?'

'How about tomorrow?'

'You don't wait for the grass to grow, do you?' she said, an appreciative grin lighting up her face.

'Strike while the iron's hot,' I replied, matching her cliché with another.

She smiled warmly. 'It's a date then. When do we start?'

'I'll come at 10:30. How's that?'

'That's fine.'

'Do you have a leather jacket?' I asked.

'Sure do.'

'Good. Wear that and jeans and closed in shoes or boots. A bike is not the place for skirts and open-toed sandals.'

'I'm glad you told me,' she replied. 'I'm looking forward to it.'

I could sense her anticipation of this new experience.

The continuing parade of food seemed to have no end but eventually it slowed down. There is only so much one can fit into a stomach. The last dish arrived; a tiramisu for each of us. Marcello arrived at the table a little while later carrying a wine glass and a chair. He sat with us and poured himself a glass of this marvellous wine.

'Was the food OK, *mia amore*?' he asked Angela.

'Superb,' she replied. She patted her stomach. 'Too much food, but too delicious to stop eating. I really loved the spicy flavour of that last pasta dish, and the aromas tickled my nose. I don't suppose you would tell me the recipe?'

'If I told you I would have to kill you. It is trade secret. But perhaps when I know you better, I might tell you a little of our big secrets.'

Angela smiled her thanks.

'Sean, *amico mio*, you look tense, and you have two policemen guarding you. What is wrong?'

'Marcello, my old chum. Someone is trying to kill me.'

43

Marcello's head lifted and he looked at me closely. His eyes sharpened, boring into my soul.

'Tell me all,' he commanded.

I knew he wouldn't allow me to shrug it off, so I briefed out the story for him.

'So, when you discover what is wrong someone will go to jail, *davvero* – that is truth?'

'Yes.'

'So, you need protection from this person?'

'You've hit the nail on the head.'

'Hit nail? What has this to do... oh, you mean, *ho ragione* – I am right. OK. I have solution. My name is Gambino. We come from Sicily.'

'Sicily?' I asked then blanched. 'The home of the Mafia?'

'Of course. We are Mafioso.'

'But you're not a thug, a crime lord?'

'You watch too many American movies. Way back Mafioso groups formed to protect the poor against oppression. My Mafioso protects our family members. You are now family, so we protect you.'

'But the police do that.'

'Police are limited. They can patrol the roads. They can find criminals after the crime, but can they protect your house before it is robbed? Do they have secret ways of finding criminals before the crime? My Mafioso can find out things the police will never find.'

I looked at him in amazement. This friendly and generous restaurateur was also Godfather to a group of underworld characters. Angela just sat there. Her mouth opened wide enough to swallow an orange whole.

'My Mafioso can protect you better than the police. Will you let us?'

'Okay,' I said, not believing that he would really be able to do much to help me. But anything was worth a try. *I'll chance my arm with this*, I thought. My Irish forebears were well known for taking chances, making decisions on the roll of a couple of dice.

'Where do we start?'

'You give me addresses, phone numbers, car registrations of people who might be hiding a secret. I have nephews and nieces who can make computers dance and sing. They are so good they will tell me what brand of toothpaste these people use, how much money they have in the bank. They will listen to phone calls. They will know who these people call and what they say. They will do things I will not tell you. They will find information the police will never find.'

'You astound me, Marcello,' I said. 'I had no idea what amazing resources you have in your family. Angela would be the best person to give you a list of names and details.'

'I'll have your list ready Monday morning,' she said. 'Give me your email address and I will send it.'

He wrote his email address on a serviette.

'Delete your email as soon as it is sent,' he said. 'We don't want anyone to find it on your computer at work. And destroy this serviette too after it is in your head.'

'Good advice,' she acknowledged.

* * *

45

We finished our meal, hugged, and thanked Marcello and walked into Norwood Parade. Our well-fed police backup team strolled slowly behind us. The street was a blaze of coloured lights. The footpaths were crowded with people from every nation. Voices babbled in a dozen or more languages and laughter mingled with music streaming from the wall-to-wall stretch of restaurants and cafes. The air was pungent with aromas from an amazing assortment of foods. Even though I had just eaten, my mouth began to water with anticipation of working my way through tangy and aromatic foods from Greek, Chinese, Indian, and Vietnamese restaurants. This was gourmet heaven.

Angela put her arm through mine and I held it captive. It felt so good to have her next to me. My heart swelled with pride. Here was I, just an ordinary guy with a beautiful woman who looked like she belonged on a catwalk. Smiles, winks, and catcalls from passing men told me all I needed to know about how lucky I was.

Eventually we returned to the car. When we reached her home, I opened her car door and walked her to the front door.

'Thanks for a great night, Sean,' she said. The tone of her voice and her beautiful smile told me she wasn't just being polite. 'Great night and great company. I'm looking forward to tomorrow.'

She reached up and kissed me gently on the cheek before disappearing into the house and closing the door.

I returned to my car, one hand touching my cheek. A smile split my face. I was so captured with my internal video of the night's events; I was surprised I managed to guide the vehicle to my home without running off the road.

I think I love that woman, I thought.

My escort followed and parked outside my house.

Chapter 7

The next morning, I disturbed Angela's neighbours with the throaty roar of the Harley's exhaust. Angela came out the door as I climbed off the machine. I took one look and lost my voice. My mouth fell open. My eyes devoured the most exquisite sight they had ever seen. She was beautiful. The leather coat and jeans emphasised her figure and the calf high boots said, *'Don't mess with me.'* Her golden hair surrounded her face like a burnished halo.

'Hi, Gorgeous,' I managed eventually to say. My tongue was still stuck halfway between complete surprise and total unbounded delight.

'Well, Big Boy,' she said, 'Let's ride.'

I had never been called Big Boy before, but I decided I liked it from her.

In my haste, I fumbled with the catches on the pannier before pulling out a spare helmet. I helped her put it on.

Once she was seated on the pillion with her feet on the pegs, I said, 'Now hold on tight and when we corner you must lean with the bike. Don't try to lean the other way.'

'Okay,' she answered a thoughtful frown on her face.

I could sense she was nervous so I planned to take it easy for a while until she relaxed, but how was I to know that those plans would be unseated very quickly, and perhaps we would be too.

I lifted the gear lever into first with my toe and gently turned the accelerator. Before taking off, I glanced in the rear-view mirror. I noticed a large dark car pulling out from the kerb and my mind went into overdrive. Was I paranoid or had I seen that car following me on my way to Angela's house? Was I being tailed? It wasn't my police escort. Where were they when I needed them?

I turned my head to speak to my passenger.

'Angela, I think we are being followed. No matter what I do, just hold on tight and remember to lean with the bike when we corner.'

I checked. The car was on our tail and closing fast. The road ahead was clear of traffic and the car pulled out to pass. I glanced and saw a window opening. My jaw dropped. A hand emerged holding a pistol.

I leaned forward, dropped my head, and flattened the bike. My tiger snarled and urged me to flee faster. We jumped from 60kph to 80kph to 100kph in seconds. I did a quick tap dance on the foot lever with my toe as we advanced through the gears. The wind on my face mask built to a tornado as we increased speed. I gripped the handlebars tightly to avoid being blown backwards off the bike. This was dangerous riding, but I had no intention of being someone's target.

My passenger gave a frightened 'Oh!' and I felt her arms tightening around my waist.

A road junction came up, so I slowed a little, leaned the bike right over and screamed around the corner, my left knee moving outwards to catch wind to pull us around the corner faster. Angela didn't fight the lean. She was a fast learner. We could have come to grief if she had leaned the wrong way.

Weaving in and out of the traffic at breakneck speed, I took turn after turn, some to the right and some to the left. This was no time to be concerned about road rules. We soon lost our tail.

We reached a more crowded part of town, so I slowed and pulled into a shopping complex carpark. I helped Angela from the bike, and she slumped against me. I held her until she recovered her balance. We found a table and I ordered coffee.

I called Ken. 'Someone just tried to shoot us.'

'You are kidding. No, you're not.' He could hear the near panic in my voice. 'Where are you?'

'Impressa Cafe in the Unley Shopping Centre.'

'Wait there. I'll be over soon.'

'Thanks, Mate,' I said.

'Did you see the gun?' I asked Angela.

'Yes,' she said. She was still in shock. Her voice trembled. 'I think I heard a bullet whizzing past my head. I was so scared. When you went fast, I was willing you to go even faster. That was the most terrifying moment of my life.'

She was babbling, words falling over words as they attempted to rid her of her terror. I let her get it all out. She needed to release her panic.

She was a gutsy lady and I told her so. She reached across the table and grasped my hand. I dredged up the best smile my tension-tightened face could muster.

'I love you, Angela, and I never want to put you through that kind of experience again.'

Her eyes opened wide in shock; a shock that helped expel some of the other demons. She tightened her grasp on my hand.

'I love you too, Sean. You have to catch these murdering swine quickly before they do any more damage.'

Ken walked to our table. He smiled at Angela then turned to me.

'Where's my coffee? What kind of a mate are you?'

'Sorry, Ken. Can't have you grumpy.'

As I walked to the counter to order his coffee, I heard him say, 'You're a game girl, Angela. I saw Sean's Harley outside, so I guessed that's how you got here.'

'Yes, Ken,' I heard her answer; 'There's never a dull moment with Sean.'

'He does seem to live life in the fast lane,' said Ken.

Angela's head bobbed in complete agreement.

'Tell me what happened,' he asked as I returned to the table.

I related our experience.

'So, you're sure you were tailed from home?' he asked.

I nodded.

'Where was your police escort?'

'No idea.'

Ken's face darkened. 'I don't suppose you got the rego number?'

I shook my head from side to side.

'Describe the vehicle.'

I did my best to recall every detail.

'Don't forget the small logo on the passenger door,' said Angela.

'You're right,' I agreed. 'Well spotted. It was a graphic of the world with a crown sitting on the top. I had forgotten that.'

'Yes,' said Angela. 'It was just below the rear-view mirror.'

'Thanks, Angela. That's helpful. Probably a stolen car, but we'll check.'

'There's one more thing, Ken. The hand holding the gun had a tattoo,' said Angela.

'You saw that?' I queried. I was astounded.

'Can you describe it for me?' asked Ken.

Angela closed her eyes. 'Let me think.'

We both looked at her in absolute awe. We held our breath, unwilling to detract her from her mind search.

She opened her eyes. 'Give me a serviette and a pen.'

I handed her a serviette and Ken pulled a pen from his pocket.

She sketched a snake's head with its mouth open, its teeth ready to bite.

'Thank you,' said Ken. 'This is valuable evidence. We'll be able the nail the guy with this. You don't know how much you've helped me,' he added.

His smile was the widest I'd ever seen on his face.

'I'm just glad I remembered,' she said.

'You don't know how glad I am,' he replied. 'This information is gold.'

He called his base and gave a description of the vehicle. 'Tell me who was on watch at Sean's house last night,' he barked into the phone. His smile disappeared rapidly. 'I want to know why they didn't notice the car following him as he left the house, and why they didn't follow.' He listened and then ordered. 'Get a car over here now,' and gave directions.

'I'll talk to your escorts from last night,' he added grimly. 'This team can tail you for the rest of the day. Don't speed or they'll book you,' he said with a grin.

'We've done enough speeding for one day.'

I smiled back at him, and Angela added her agreement.

'I'll meet you at the winery tomorrow morning. We need to solve this case quickly,' said Ken. He left us as the police car he had ordered pulled into the park.

I gave my hand to Angela to help her from her seat. Not that I thought she needed any help. I just wanted to hold her hand again.

'Let's go for that ride with our escort.'

'Okay,' she answered. 'I feel safer now. I must say I've never felt happy before about having the boys in blue behind my vehicle, but suddenly it's comforting.'

We set off, more sedately than we had arrived. The ride up the highway and through the hills was relaxing and stimulating, both at the same time. The blue skies made an excellent background to the green hills and drops of dew on the gum leaves sparkled like fairy lights.

Further along, the autumn colours rolled out like a magic carpet. I felt Angela loosen her grip around my waist. She was relaxing and floating with the bike's movement like riding a floating mattress on a gentle sea.

She leaned forward so she could speak close to my ear. 'This is wonderful, Sean. I never realised how close to nature you can feel on a bike.'

I kept rigidly to the speed limit and the blue car kept three car lengths behind. *Good driving, guys,* I thought. *And thanks for watching our backs.* The double entendre tickled my sense of the ridiculous.

We had a great lunch and held hands over final coffee as we sat chatting.

'How about we go to mine so I can grab some clothes and my toothbrush before I take you home?'

'Sounds good to me.'

She smiled warmly and tightened her grip on my hands. 'That's what I want very much. Let's get riding, Big Boy.'

My heart was bursting with love for this wonderful woman. I didn't want this day ever to end. I called the troops from their lunch, told them our plan, and suggested they talk to Ken about surveillance that evening. No doubt he would be pleased he only needed to mount one team instead of two.

We took a different route home through some of the spreading farmland to the south of the freeway before returning to the city. A day that had begun disastrously had turned into the best day of my life.

Chapter 8

The following day, Angela and I helped Ken and his team set up the incident room to continue their questioning. He had finished with the winemaking team and was now beginning with the administration staff.

I left to begin my own investigations. Firstly, I approached the accountant. His portly body was half hidden behind two computer screens surrounded by mountains of paper files.

'Good morning, Mr. Douglas,' I greeted, 'I would like to inspect the General Ledger and Payroll records this week. Can you help me get access?'

'It's not convenient this week,' he snarled from his downturned mouth. His bleak eyes regarded me as if I was a noxious pest.

'Oh? Why is that?' I asked politely.

'We are running end-of-month routines this week,' he said abruptly. 'We won't be finished before Friday evening.'

He turned back to his desk in a clear statement of dismissal.

'Well, what about Payroll?' I asked.

He lifted a stony face from his paperwork. 'It's also pay week so, as I said before, it's not convenient.'

I dug my heels in. I wasn't going to take this brush off easily. 'Who can I talk to about access to the systems,' I asked pointedly.

'Clerical pool,' was his final and very conclusive statement. He closed his mouth like a trap grabbing the leg of a fox. With his head he signalled that I should leave by the door instantly if not sooner.

That got my Irish up. Smiling a wide, false smile and delaying my exit, I said in my sweetest tones, 'Thank you Mr Douglas, I'll look forward to another illuminating chat next Monday morning. I'm sure you will be only too pleased to help me with my audit then.'

I turned and walked slowly and deliberately from his office whistling a jaunty sea shanty.

You're hiding something Mate, I thought. *You have just moved up my list to number one suspect.*

I went to find Angela.

'Have you sent the list to Marcello yet?'

'Just getting it ready now,' she said.

'Move Mr Bless-His-Heart Steve Douglas to the top of the list. He has just given me the brush off and I believe he's hiding something,' I said.

'Why? What went wrong?' she asked.

'He refused to let me see the General Ledger files. Muttered some excuse about running end-of-month reports,' I replied.

'Perhaps he had a good reason?'

'I'm sure he had a good reason. Good for him and not good for me. I wouldn't be surprised if he is trying to fiddle the books before I see them.'

'That sounds awful, Sean. Surely he couldn't be that bad.'

'You're very kind-hearted, my love, but someone is stealing a lot of money and he's in a very good position to be able to do that. Let Marcello's crew check him out. I'm going to try to get into those records another way.'

'OK. I'll put him at the top of the list,' she agreed.

I went to find the clerical pool manager, Mrs Moore. I discovered quickly that she was a mother chook with her girls in the typing pool. She was their boss and made sure they kept their noses to the grindstone, but she was also their Agony Aunt, helping them through personal problems.

'Hullo, young man,' she said in welcome, 'How can I help you?'

'I'd like access to the accounting software,' I said. 'The accountant is too busy to help me this week.'

'Stevie Boy is a bit of a stuffed shirt,' she commented. 'He doesn't go out of his way to help anyone. Come with me, Ducky.'

She took my arm and pulled me into a close encounter with her ample body. The warm and spicy sweet odour of Lancôme Trésor reminded me of my mother. She led me to her office.

'You can use my computer. I'm already logged in, so you don't need a password.'

'Many thanks, Mrs Moore,' I said. I was pleased to receive her immediate and friendly assistance.

'Call me Nancy, love,' she clucked and walked back to her little chicks.

I sat at her computer and followed the prompts to the general ledger files. I knew that if I didn't download or change any data, I wouldn't interfere with the end-of-month reporting.

Soon I was following the trail of transactions and making notes. Hours later nothing out of the ordinary had shown up. I had plenty more checking to do, but I had done enough for one day.

The next day I went back to the typing pool and spend another laborious day checking the accounting files. I couldn't find anything suspicious, but I did find a few inefficient procedures that could be tightened up. I made a list for my report to David.

Then something caught my eye. The date stamp on some of the entries carried yesterday's date. *'Why were entries being made while they were running end-of-month?'* I checked carefully. All those changes related to payroll.

Why alter payroll entries, I wondered.

I scanned through the payroll files, but nothing seemed out of the ordinary. I printed the information from the computer screen. *Where to now?* No immediate questions occurred to me.

'Nancy,' I asked. 'These records only show the last three months. Where are older records stored?

'Oh. I think they do a print run and store them in the cellar.'

'What about electronic files?'

'They are stored off site. I don't know where.'

'Where is the cellar?' I asked.

She smiled, obviously pleased to be able to help me. 'It's under the Boardroom. I think they used to store wine there in the old days.'

'Who has the key?'

'David should have that,' she replied. 'Go and ask him.'

I strode to David's office where Angela met me at the door.

'Hi Angel,' I said. 'Do you know where to find the key to the cellar?'

'Why do you want to go to that dark, smelly place?' she asked. Her curiosity was aroused.

'I believe the old accounting files are kept there,' I replied.

'Oh. I'll get the key for you.'

'Thanks, and then show me where the door is.'

'OK. Won't be a minute.'

She darted into David's office and returned a few moments later clutching a bunch of ancient keys.

'Come with me,' she said, leading me down the corridor.

We reached an old oak door. Its age was etched into its timbers like wrinkles on an old face. Angela chose one of the large, darkened keys that looked like it could open an ancient treasure chest. She inserted it in the lock and struggled to turn it. I put my hand over hers and together we unlocked the door. I gazed into a dark forbidding interior. Angela found a light switch and old globes cast a feeble glow over a steep rickety set of stairs leading down into the dark depths.

'There are more light switches at the bottom,' Angela explained. 'Be careful you don't lose your balance and slip.'

'I'll be careful,' I promised and began my descent. Angela went back to her work.

I took my time going down the precarious steps, taking one at a time, and reaching backwards to steady my descent by holding earlier steps. There was no handrail.

At the bottom I could see nothing at all. It seemed like I had reached the centre of the earth ... or Hades my overactive mind suggested. I felt around the walls and eventually located a bank of light switches. I activated them all and saw around me endless racks that had obviously been constructed to hold bottles of wine. They now supported box after box of files.

Luckily the boxes were labelled and dated. I walked along row after row until I found the latest, a box stamped with the current year. I carried the box to a table and opened it. I reached into my pocket and took out the printed list of staff I had copied from the payroll records. I placed that to one side of the table so I could compare it with older records.

At first glance everything seemed in order. The most recent records seemed to tally with my screen dump. As I worked back through the records, I could see the total salary payments each fortnight was slowly decreasing.

The trend continued backwards as far as I could go with this box.

I went back to the shelves and retrieved the previous box. The decreasing total salary bill each fortnight continued for a further six months then plateaued. I worked forward again, calculating the increased amounts as a percentage of the base.

It could be due to Cost Price Index increases, I first thought. But I soon realised the increases were way above any change in the CPI. *Why was the winery increasing wages to this extent?* Then I kicked myself mentally. Of course! The wage bill was increasing because they were hiring more staff.

I returned to the earlier records and did a head count. I checked the head count on my printed staff list and did my sums. The winery was increasing its staff numbers by around four or five people a month and had been doing this for over a year.

Does David realise, I thought, that he is increasing staff numbers beyond what the budget can afford. This is where his profits are disappearing. Too many staff.

I felt happy that I had finally discovered the cause of his financial woes.

I sorted out the financial records I needed to prove my point and packed the others back in the boxes. I replaced the boxes on the shelves and walked towards the stairs, a bundle of papers under my arm.

Suddenly the door above slammed shut. I jumped with surprise. A few moments later the lights went out. *What is going on?* I thought. I was left standing somewhere near the stairs in pitch darkness. Not a glimmer of light showed anywhere.

I suddenly became aware of the coldness of this black atmosphere, and I shivered. Fear coursed through my body. I listened carefully hardly daring to breath. My tiger emerged from my super consciousness. His head rotated, nose, ears and eyes sensing the space, searching for a threat. Was there someone here? My heart thumped. My breathing became shallow. Was this another attempt on my life?

Nothing stirred.

I remembered my mobile phone had a torch app. I felt in the dark and found the phone in my coat pocket. I switched on the app and a small glow lit up my immediate vicinity. I swivelled the phone around me to see if I was alone. Nothing moved in the circle of light from the phone screen. I moved to the wall and tried the light switches. They were still on. It seemed someone had cut the power supply to this cellar at the meter box.

I'll call Angela, I decided.

I selected her number and attempted to call. *Damn. No signal.*

I listened carefully for any movement, desperately hoping that Angela would come back. My mobile battery was almost spent. I wasn't game to try to climb those rickety stairs with no light. No doubt someone hoped I would try to climb and slip and break my neck.

It seemed hours before I heard the door open.

'Sean. Are you there?' Angela called.

Relief flooded my system.

'Yes, Honey. Someone turned off the power at the meter box. Can you check it, please? I'm not climbing these stairs in the dark.'

'Okay. Back soon,' she called.

A few minutes later the lights came on again. I breathed a sigh of relief and climbed the stairs slowly clutching my bundle of papers.

'Boy, I'm glad you checked. I could have been there all night,' I said. 'I was sure I'd be eaten by rats.'

'I was worried. I didn't know where you were. When I saw the cellar door closed, I thought you must have finished so I searched everywhere for you. Trying the cellar was my very last hope.'

'I've never been so glad to hear your voice,' I said, 'There was no signal down there for my phone so I couldn't call you. Is David still here?'

'No, he left half an hour ago.'

'Oh well. I'll have some good news for him tomorrow.'

'By the way,' said Angela. 'I saw someone hurrying down the corridor a little while ago. It's unusual for staff to be here so late.'

'Could you identify the person?' I asked

'Sorry. No. It was only a brief glimpse.'

I sighed with frustration. Knowing who was hurrying away would be a valuable piece of information.

* * *

Soon after returning home, my phone rang.

'Sean, we need more people to check,' said Marcello.

'What have you found?' I asked.

'Lots. The accountant, he is, how you say, bad tempered, rude, demanding. His wife she should put poison in his coffee. He has no friends. Makes no phone calls. Nothing. He goes to work. He comes home, shouts at his wife and watches TV. But we will keep watching him. We think he could kill. We also found he has a lot of money in the bank and in shares.'

'Yes. Please keep him on your watch list. His behaviour at the winery is suspicious.'

'Bene.'

'What about Nancy Moore?'

'She is friendly. Always on phone. She talks to family, friends. She listens. She gives advice about babies, children, boyfriends. She is Earth Mother. She is no criminal.'

'And John Cartwright?'

'Talks all the time. Rotary. Plans. Raising money for charity. Helping people. Nothing for us.'

'OK, Marcello. Thank you. We have two more people for you to check. They are Marie Young the head of Human Resources, and her support person Adrian Chow the payroll clerk. Angela will send you details tomorrow. Let's hope we have more luck with these.'

'Take care *amico. Ciao.*'

Chapter 9

Early the next morning I went straight to David's office, my pile of papers in my hand.

I was about to knock on the door when Karl Amos appeared.

'Sean,' he called loudly.

I turned, surprised to see him away from his area.

'Tony asked me to bring you down to the winemaking area quickly. There is a problem you might be able to solve for us.'

'I can come after I see David.'

I noticed a quick glance at the papers in my hand.

'No time for that. We need you immediately.'

He grabbed my arm and began shepherding me down the corridor at a fast pace. I was literally being dragged along in his wake.

'Wait, Karl,' I almost shouted, partly from panic. 'Surely it can wait a few moments.'

'Come on,' he urged. 'Nearly there now.'

As we rounded a corner and entered the wide doorway into the winemaking area, the noise of whirring pumps, rattling bottles, shouts, and forklifts racing hither and yon filled the air with a cacophonous riot. I stumbled as Karl yanked me towards the platform in the centre where Tony stood. He saw me, waved, and beckoned me with his hand. I half waved back with the arm that still clutched a pile of papers. Karl still had the other in a firm grip.

Suddenly Tony's face changed from surprise to panic. He called but I couldn't hear his words. Then his arms danced a crazy sideways *pas de deux*.

I glanced over my shoulder. A heavily laden forklift was headed straight for me. The driver was obscured from my view by a bright light that momentarily blinded me. *Shit!* I thought. I closed my eyes. My panic was broken by a loud snarl from my tiger. He urged me to jump sideways. My eyes opened wide. Papers flew from my arm in an untidy cloud as I make the leap of a lifetime. I squeezed into a niche between the large round fermentation tank and a 300-litre oak barrel. A faint recollection from my past of an Irish priest saying the *Last Rites* in Latin flashed across my mind. '... *Pater, Filius et Spiritús Sancti...*' My heart raced and a tremble travelled down my frozen body. I didn't take a breath until I heard the forklift race off. It was only then that I remembered Karl's hand leaving my arm just a mere second before the incident.

He came over to me brushing dust off his shirt.

'That was a close one,' he called. 'Are you okay?'

I looked at him in complete disbelief and struggled to my feet. 'My papers. I need my papers.'

'Forget them,' he said, 'Your life is more important than a few mouldy old papers.'

How do you know they are mouldy and old? is the question I should have asked but I didn't think of that until later.

'Why are we here?' is the question I did ask.

'Let me help you up then we can ask Tony,' he replied.

He pulled me ungainly to my feet and hustled me up the stairs.

Tony helped brush me down.

'Who was driving that forklift?' Tony asked Karl.

'Sorry, Tony. In the panic of the moment, I didn't catch sight of the driver.'

'Make some enquiries, please. See if you can identify him. He's too dangerous to be working here.'

'Yes, I will,' said Karl before bounding down the platform steps two at a time. He seemed anxious to be anywhere else but on that platform.

When he had gone, I turned to Tony. 'What was so important I had to be rushed here as if the place was burning down?'

He looked at me strangely. 'I'm puzzled. I just asked Karl to mention I would like to see you sometime today. There was no immediate rush.'

'But he hurried me down here at a run because he said you needed to see me urgently.'

'It was only about some anomalies in our wine records. It can wait... He hurried you down here?'

I nodded. His eyes stared at me, but his thoughts were somewhere else. 'I wonder...'

'Wonder what?' I prompted.

'Nothing ... yet.' His mind was still somewhere else.

My thoughts were somewhere else too. Had he really asked Karl to find me immediately? Had Karl decided that I needed to be brought down immediately? Was the forklift incident accidental or planned? If planned, by whom? Was there any link to the papers I was carrying?

'My papers,' I remembered.

'Are they important?'

'Very.'

He led me down the stairs and helped me retrieve as many of the papers as we could. Some had blown away. Others had landed in the large wine vat and were rapidly becoming unreadable.

At that moment a running policeman appeared.

'We didn't know where you had gone,' he gasped.

I didn't say anything about him being busy chatting up the secretarial staff, but I would have words with Ken later.

He helped retrieve the last of the papers.

'I must take these to David straight away.'

'I'll come with you. We don't want any more incidents like this one,' said Tony.

I looked at him sideways. Was this a genuine offer or did he have an ulterior agenda? Could I trust anyone anymore?

The three of us trooped back to David's office in silence. I brushed my companions aside as I entered the doorway.

I found David alone in his office, so I walked in and closed the door behind me.

'I found where your profits are disappearing, David,' I said.

'Where?'

'You're hiring too many staff.'

'What do you mean?'

'You've been hiring four or five extra staff members each month for more than twelve months.'

'Who says I have?'

'The payroll records.'

'Show me.'

'I've just had an incident with a forklift...'

He raised his eyebrows in question, but I waved my hands to indicate he should wait for an explanation.

'Later,' I said.

'...so, some of the pages are missing, but we can recover them from the electronic backup files. There will be enough here to show the story.'

I unrolled the bundle of papers I had retrieved from the cellar and spread them on his desk. I showed him the monthly increases in the total payroll bill. David's face went a deathly white.

'My God,' he said. He grasped the desk for support. 'We haven't been hiring extra people. The staff numbers have been steady all that time. The money has been disappearing into wages for non-existent staff. Where is it now?'

He sat back heavily in his chair. 'Sean. Help me out. How do we ...?'

'... solve this mystery,' I supplied. 'Let's keep quiet about this while we make further enquiries. We know from the murder last week that there could be at least two people involved. Maybe more. We don't want to spook them. I'll keep investigating and pretend to be looking everywhere except at payroll. I'll see if I can devise a double blind. We want to catch these people and get the money back. We could be talking of a figure approaching a couple of million dollars or more.'

'That is the kind of figure I believe we have lost.'

'Meanwhile, David, can you hide these papers in your safe?'

'Yes. I'll do that right away. Now tell me about the forklift incident.'

I sketched out the event in the winemaking area.

'I don't know whether it was accidental or deliberate, but it scared the pants off me. If it was deliberate, then either Karl Amos or Tony Antenucci could be involved. Neither of them seems likely to be involved in something like this … but you never know.'

'I would find it hard to believe either of them is involved,' said David, 'but as you say, you never know.'

'One last thing, David. Can you organise for me to see the backup electronic files? I need full details.'

'I'll organise it straight away. Perhaps you can call in on your way here tomorrow. They have their office in Magill. Not too far off your path.'

'Thank you. Can you please give the address to Angela?'

'Certainly.'

Angela caught up with me as I left David's office. As she arrived, Tony turned and walked briskly in the direction of the winery. The policeman moved to stand with his back to the wall, watching up and down the corridor as if at a tennis match.

'I've been looking for you.'

I smiled. 'You've found me.'

'Don't be an ass. I was worried. I had a premonition that something was wrong.'

'I wish you had that premonition earlier this morning then I would have stayed in bed.'

'Why?'

'I was nearly squashed by a forklift.'

Her face blanched. Her hands went to her mouth. 'Spill it,' she managed to squeeze out between tension-tightened lips.

I sketched out the incident for her. 'Can you email Marcello and ask him to get his team to check out Karl Amos and Tony Antenucci.'

'Not Tony,' she said. 'He's the most honest person I know. And Karl has always seemed straight too.'

'That's the way I have read them too. But this morning's incident worries me and suggests one or both may be involved. We need to have them checked out to be sure they aren't involved.'

My phone rang insistently.

'Hullo?'

'I have a report for you,' said Marcello.

'Go ahead.'

'Your Chinese man is interesting,'

'You mean Adrian Chow?'

'Who else? Some of his family members belong to a Chinese Triad.'

'Crooks you mean?'

'*Si*. They lend money at exorbitant rates and do some drug peddling on the side.'

'Do they murder?'

'Yes. But only with traditional Chinese Ring dagger.'

'Not beating people to death with a blunt instrument?'

'No *mio fratello*, no blunt instruments.'

'What about Adrian?'

'He seems clean, but we keep him on our list. Now your friend Marie Young …'

Angela grabbed my arm and turned me so I could see David approaching at a fast pace.

'Sorry Marcello. I'm being called to talk with David. I'll call you later. Angela is about to send you two more names. *Ciao*.'

I closed my phone and turned to Angela. I was about to remind her to email Marcello when she said, 'Okay I'll contact Marcello. Where will I find you?'

I smiled and said, 'Reading my mind, are you?'

'Your mind is an open book to me.'

I stored that comment in my mind for an interesting conversation later, perhaps over a glass of wine.

'After I talk with David, I'll go back to work on Nancy's computer. I'll be safe there.'

'I'll come and check on you again in a little while. I don't want any more of those premonitions.'

David began talking before he reached me.

'Sean, can you please tell me again how the double blind you are proposing will work. I was so distraught when we spoke before, I didn't listen carefully, and I don't want to do or say anything that will contradict what you are doing.'

'Sure, David,' I responded. I went through the steps I was taking again.

'Thank you, Sean. I have it now. No word about payroll.'

'Exactly.'

He turned to retrace his steps back to his office.

I returned to Nancy's area. 'Hi Nancy, can I borrow your computer again? I need to start checking insurances.'

I knew Nancy talked to everyone and she was the ideal leak for my bogus plan.

'Yes, of course, young man. You are very welcome. Insurances did you say?'

'That's right. I need to find out how many insurance policies there are and how much we spend on them each year. After that I'll be looking at how much wine of each variety is in storage.'

'I'll get one of the girls to bring you a cup of coffee. How does that sound?'

'It sounds stupendous,' I replied, a big smile stretching across my face. 'You are so helpful. If you weren't already attached, I think I'd marry you.'

Her smile wrapped around her body. It captured the warmth of her total being.

'I think Angela might have a word or two to say about that,' she warned, shaking her finger at me.

'Well, perhaps you would be my second choice.'

I knew how to get this person on side. She was the ideal spreader of misinformation.

Meanwhile I checked her computer for the names of all staff members in the records and which departments they worked in. I copied the list to my phone. I didn't want any paper records that might give away my real intentions. Then I printed a list of all insurance policies and their premiums and left that on Nancy's desk next to her computer where she would find it.

I walked out to the winemaking area to find Tony Antenucci. He had been so helpful previously I had to trust him.

'Tony,' I asked. 'Can I trust you to keep a secret?'

'I'll be as quiet as the grave.'

'Let's hope it doesn't come to that,' I replied. 'You know I've been helping the police with their investigation into the death of the Circus Performer.'

'Yes.'

He stood quietly waiting for me to reveal what was on my mind.

'We think he was murdered by at least one and possibly two people who work here, and we believe if the investigation doesn't help us find them, the winery may go bankrupt and you and everyone else will lose their jobs.'

Tony gasped. 'That serious?' His hands reached for the railing of the platform above the large wine fermentation tank. His body sagged.

'Yes. Tony, I am going to ask you to do something for me and it must remain our secret. No one else must discover what we are discussing. No one! If anybody asks, we have been talking about how much wine of each variety is in storage.'

'How much wine is in storage?'

'Exactly. In fact, I want you to get help from your staff in compiling a complete report of varieties, quantities, and length of time before bottling. Tell them it is for my report to the board. Leave copies around so that they can see it is a genuine report.'

'That can be done quite quickly.'

'Don't hurry it. But that is not what I really need. This second task must remain a tight secret.'

'What is it?' he asked softly.

'I want a list of the names and positions of everyone who works in the winemaking area, including machine operators, bottling and warehouse staff, and delivery staff as well. Include everyone who spends much time in your winemaking area, even those that come from the front office like Angela.'

'You don't suspect her, do you?'

'Not at all, but I have a good reason for knowing everyone who visits staff in this area regularly, and who they visit.'

'This is to be a secret?'

'Yes. I have a very good reason for asking you to keep this second report from everyone in the winery, even from those you think you can trust. In time I will explain to you why it must be kept a secret. I want you to compile this second report away from the winery. Do it at home this weekend and email it to me at my home when it is complete. Don't keep copies anywhere and delete the email from your home computer when it has been sent. Are you fine with all that?'

'Yes. I will do as you say. But I will have many questions for you when you are able to speak openly.'

'With your help, Tony, that should be very soon. I am very much in your debt. I need your help more than I can tell you.'

'Okay, Sean. I will do what I can.'

I didn't tell him that I would be double-checking his information just in case he was involved with the theft of company money. I liked the police phrase "...to eliminate him from our enquiries" – or had I learned that from TV murder mysteries?

Chapter 10

Saturday afternoon I called Marcello.

'*Mio fratello*. What is happening?'

'The stalkers are back, and we will be going out tomorrow morning.'

'Do you think the stalkers will try to shoot you again?' he asked.

'I'd put money on it,' I replied.

'So, we need a plan to catch them. What time will you leave the house tomorrow?'

I looked at Angela. 'This lovely lady wants to take me somewhere special for lunch so I guess we will leave around 11:00am. It's her secret.'

Angela nodded. I could see she was delighted with her surprise. She was almost jumping up and down with excitement, so I knew it was important to her. Her hair swished around her head like a golden shower.

'Give me your address and be ready to leave a few minutes before. Back the car from the house at exactly 11:00am. Organise your Detective friend to bring some armed police and arrive at exactly 2 minutes past 11. Is your police guard still outside your house?'

'Yes.'

'Get the police watching your house to drive away at 10:30 and hide around the corner. Tell them to come back one-minute past 11 and drive in front of the stalkers' car.'

'What are you planning?' I asked. I was amazed he had come up with a plan in such a short time. There were depths to this man that I would love to plumb at another time.

'That is my secret. You will be impressed, and the stalkers will be caught and taken to jail. Just make sure the police keep to time.'

'Thank you, Marcello. You are a mate like no other. I'm astounded at what you have just organised. I'll call Ken and make sure he understands what is going to happen. Thank you for a most amazing meal the other night.'

Angela grabbed the phone from me. 'Thank you from the bottom of my heart for that delicious meal,' she said. 'Next time I see you I will give you a big kiss.'

'*Buona sera*,' he said quietly. 'Go with God.'

* * *

Sunday morning arrived. I walked out to collect the morning paper that had been delivered in the early hours. I looked across the street and waved to the surveillance team in the police car. I glanced up the street and noted the dark grey vehicle against the kerb. There were two males in the front seats. I walked back inside.

'Our stalkers are back,' I said. I inclined my head to indicate their direction. 'I'll call Marcello, Ken and the surveillance guys to put our plan into action.'

I picked up my phone and dialled. 'Good morning, Marcello. Our unwanted guests are back. Are you ready to put your plan into action?'

'The Mafioso is ready for battle,' he said. 'You will be ready for 11:00am?'

'We'll be ready. *Ciao* Mate.' I hung up and dialled Ken.

'Plan *Catchthebuggers* is on. See you and your team at 11.02am.'

'Okay,' he said. 'Hope your Italian mate knows what he is doing.'

'I'm sure he does,' I replied. I mentioned nothing about the Mafia connections. That would create problems Marcello didn't need.

I called the surveillance team in the car across the street. 'You guys ready to pretend to disappear at 10.30? Don't forget to return at 11.01 and park across the front of the stalkers' car.'

'Yes, Sean. Looking forward to it.'

A little before 11.00am I backed the car from the garage into the drive so the stalkers could see we were preparing to leave. I left the motor running and went back inside for Angela.

'Ready, my love?' I asked.

'Ready as I'll ever be,' she replied. 'I just hope we don't get shot at again. That's more than I can handle.'

We walked out to the car and looked up the street in amazement. A large group of youths was advancing down the street. They rode motor bikes, they rode motorised scooters, they rode bicycles, or they rode skateboards. There must have been fifty or more of them in a dense and determined army of teenagers, spread right across the street from footpath to footpath. I narrowed my gaze to watch the advance. They took on the appearance in my mind of a phalanx of Roman legionnaires; shields held up and short swords at the ready.

As I backed out into the street, they reached our gate and parted to let me through before closing ranks again. A tall lad in the centre shouted and they stopped, totally blocking the street. They started pushing and shoving each other, shouting, gesturing, and taking no notice of bystanders or traffic. The stalkers edged away from the kerb to tail us but were stopped by the mob.

I parked the car and we got out to watch.

The surveillance police vehicle appeared from around a corner with a screech of tyres. Brakes squealed as it pulled up, blocking the front of the stalkers' car. A moment later a Star Force Special Operations team pulled up behind the vehicle and men jumped out with weapons at the ready. They pulled open the front doors and dragged the occupants into the street. The two thugs were pushed up against the car, handcuffed and patted down. A quick search of the vehicle revealed several weapons.

Two minutes later not a single teenager was to be seen in the street.

I drove back to meet Ken. He was talking with the *Star Force* Commander.

'We've found weapons and I'm sure we'll find the car is stolen.'

'Loitering with intent, do you think?' asked Ken.

'At the very least, but there'll be more. I've seen mug shots of both these characters at the station.'

'Just a minute. Let me look at their hands,' he commanded.

As he walked over, he pulled the serviette with Angela's drawing from his pocket. He walked behind the two men who were still straddled against their car. The weaselly one had a tattoo on his hand matching the sketch. The snake's head on his hand was unmistakable. The body snaked its way up and around his arm.

'Got you!' said Ken with a satisfied smile. 'This one's the gunman. We've got him on attempted murder at least. The other one is his accomplice. Read them their rights, then lock 'em up tight and get that vehicle to Forensics. Get the guys to go over it with a fine-tooth comb.'

Ken walked over to us.

'You can go out and enjoy yourselves. No more shooting incidents today. Thank you, Angela. One of those guys has the tattoo you drew for us. And thank that Italian mate of yours, Sean. His crew did a great job. Perhaps we could hire some of them as police cadets.'

'I'll suggest that to Marcello. I'm not too sure his family would see that positively, but you never know.'

Angela and I returned to our vehicle. She collapsed into the passenger seat with a loud sigh of relief. 'Thank goodness that is over. We won't be shot at again, will we?'

'Not today,' I replied. 'Ken will make sure those two are locked up tight. I hope he can get them to say who hired them. I'll bet it was one of the people we are trying to identify for the winery problems.'

'Let's go and enjoy ourselves then,' said Angela. A small smile began to play with the corners of her mouth.

I glanced at her to check that she was really beginning to relax. I smiled for the first time that day.

We set off with our surveillance team following three car lengths behind.

Chapter 11

'Where are we off to, Angel?' I asked.

'After all that excitement, the rest of the day will seem dull for you,' she said.

'Not at all. I'll be with you with no more death threats hanging over my head; at least for today.'

'Okay. Head towards Kensington Road,' she commanded. 'I'll tell you when to stop.'

We were just passing a Sports Stadium when she shouted, 'Stop!'

'What? Here? But we didn't wear our sports togs.'

'You'll manage,' she replied in a quietly determined voice.

We walked to the main door, and I was astounded to see the stadium full of trestle tables and chairs. People stood in groups talking. None of them was wearing sports togs. Some had taken seats at tables.

'What's happening here?' I was totally mystified.

'This is my surprise,' she said, smiling at my confusion. 'It's an Indian banquet and you will meet some of my friends.'

'Indian banquet in a Sports stadium? Now I've seen everything.'

'Not yet you haven't, Big Boy. I have a few more surprises up my sleeve.'

She was toying with me in a playful manner. I didn't mind in the least, but I couldn't let her know that too soon. We were developing an almost intoxicating playful manner between us. I loved it, and I loved her for it.

'Come with me,' she said as she took my arm.

We walked towards a group of people to one side of the hall. I could see eight people. I had already noticed that each table had ten seats. They were all about our age. As we approached, their conversation stopped as they turned to welcome us. I was introduced around the group and tried hard to remember names as I shook their hands. The four guys were open and welcoming. The women were more appraising. Their eyes narrowed as they looked me up and down. It was obvious that they wanted to be sure Angela's new man was good enough for her.

Soon a gong sounded and a middle-aged Indian man in ceremonial costume asked us to go to our tables. He explained that the banquet was a smorgasbord where we could help ourselves to any of the dishes that were arranged around the walls of the hall. We could go back as many times as we liked. I took a quick look around the walls and noticed large signs indicating the different menu items. He explained that this month the food was representative of dishes found in the Punjab area in northern India and he gave a brief explanation of the spices commonly used in that area and the types of dishes to be found.

'You may be aware,' he said, 'that the most popular way of cooking in the Punjab is in a tandoor oven. We hired several gas-fired tandoor ovens for today's event. We have old favourites like Tandoori chicken and Naan bread, both made in a tandoor. We also have some of the rich buttery stews such as Rogan Josh, Butter Chicken and Chicken Tikka. The Punjabis love adding ginger, turmeric and chilli so be prepared for some highly spiced dishes. I'm sure you will enjoy their mango chutney, one of my favourites. All those dishes can be eaten with Basmati rice or naan bread.'

'Do they have sweets?' asked a lady in the front row of tables.

'My word, yes,' said our host, 'Among the deserts offered to you today we have Kulfi, an ice-cream-like dessert, Malpua and Halva, which some people say is the food of the Gods. You might also like to drink some Lassi which you would probably call buttermilk. Enjoy your meal and you may go back for more food as often as you like. *Anand Lena*, enjoy!

'Come on.' Angela grabbed my arm. 'Let's get our first course.'

We walked along the tables reading the labels and looking at the food. We chose some finger food items for our entrée and returned to the table.

'I saw a police car following you into the park,' said one of the men. 'Speeding fine?'

'Nothing like that,' Angela answered. 'We were riding on Sean's Harley the other day and we were shot at. The police are there to protect us.'

'Shot at?' exclaimed one of the women. 'Tell us more.'

Angela briefly described the event. Mouths dropped open all around the table.

'But what is this about?' asked another woman.

'Sean has been investigating why our winery has been losing money. Someone doesn't want him to find the reason.'

'This is extraordinary,' said the woman. 'Nothing like this happens in our dull lives.'

'Just as well,' said her husband. 'You ride a Harley?' he asked of Sean. His tone displayed his envy.

'Yes. It's one of my passions.'

'Don't even think about it,' his wife said loudly.

Everyone at the table laughed. We could see the hackles rising up her neck.

'But I've got a nice bonus coming next month. I'm tempted. Then we could go riding with Sean and Angela.'

'And get shot at?' his wife retorted.

He raised his eyes to the ceiling in mock anguish.

'Did you say the New Age winery,' asked one of the other guys.

'Yes. Do you know it?' I asked.

'Know it! I manage the accounts for that winery at my bank in Magill,' said Frank.

'You do?' My interest grew rapidly. 'Can I come and talk with you about the bank accounts?' I asked.

'You are more than welcome. Just call and make an appointment with my secretary, Sally. I'll warn her that you will call, and I'll ask her to fast track the appointment.'

'Thank you, Frank. I'll call early next week. You may be able to answer a few questions I have about the bank statements.'

'Only too happy to assist if I can,' replied Frank.

I sighed with relief. Some of my concerns could soon be answered.

'Excuse me for a moment,' I said rising from the table. 'I need to speak to the maître de.'

I walked across to the Indian guy in the fancy suit.

'Excuse me,' I said. 'There are two policemen outside waiting to guide us home and I would like to buy some food for them.'

'No worries, Sir,' he said. 'We have plenty of food. Would you like me to select an assortment of dishes and have them taken to your police escort?'

'I would. Thank you. How much will that be?'

'Nothing, Sir. It will be on the house. We are always pleased to look after the police. We sometimes need their protection. I will include our takeaway menu for next time they are near our restaurant.'

I thanked him and walked back to the table.

'What was all that about?' Angela enquired.

'I just organised some food for our police friends outside.'

'Oh, Sean. You are so thoughtful. That's one of the things I love about you,' she said. Her face broke into a wide smile, and she sent me an air kiss.

Knowing nods and smiles went around the table. I had earned a few brownie points with Angela's friends. I felt very comfortable. They would soon become my friends too.

Chapter 12

We arrived at the winery early the next morning, accompanied by our police escort. I went straight to the accountant's office and walked in unannounced.

'Good morning, Mr Douglas,' I said.

He gave a brief grudging acknowledgement of my presence. It may have been a poorly formed smile but appeared much more like a scowl.

'What do you want?' struggled from his lips.

'What I need to do today is audit the General Ledger,' I answered. 'I can do it in your office, or elsewhere, but I need you to organise a username and password with full access rights.'

'I told you the other day. Go to the Clerical pool.'

'I approached them, but they are asking for your permission to give me full access rights. This is the normal way these transactions are done, as I'm sure you are aware.'

'Don't speak to me as if I am the Village Idiot!' he exploded.

I kept calm as I said, 'Like you, I have to operate within a carefully scripted professional code. I am trying to do my job by the book. I would prefer to work with your knowledge and support. If there is a reason for me to choose another approach, I ask you to advise me right away.'

He gulped and his face grew red. His blood pressure rose rapidly. Obviously not many people called his bluff. He grabbed a pad and scribbled a quick note. He held the note up and I grabbed it from his hand before he reconsidered.

'Thank you,' I said cheerfully. 'I'll take this to the Clerical Pool, shall I?'

He gave a curt nod so I turned and walked from his office quickly to avoid any object that might fly through the air towards the back of my head.

I went straight to the Clerical Pool.

'Good morning, Nancy,' I greeted my friend from last week. 'Guess what I've got?'

I showed her the note.

'Mr Douglas has given his permission for you to organise my access to the company financial accounts.'

Her mouth and eyes opened wide with astonishment.

'You got Stevie boy to authorise this? My hat goes off to you. You are the first to ever get him to back down. It must be that Irish tongue of yours. Congratulations.'

She quickly organised my access to the system under my own username and password. I would need that if I had to present information from the company accounts in a court of law. She also organised a computer and printer for me to use in the office next to hers. I asked her to locate a filing cabinet that I could lock. I had deliberately asked for a position near her because I knew she and her team of chicks would inform me if anyone tried to see what I was working on.

I photocopied Douglas's note to retain a record. Every piece of evidence would need to be kept safe. The accountant was still a strong suspect for both theft and murder. But who could be working with him? There were still many questions that needed answers.

I set to work in earnest printing reports from the accounts and payroll databases.

* * *

The rest of the week passed quickly as I completed my auditing. The final Audit Report was scheduled for the next Friday.

Tuesday I was working on my report when Sarah arrived at my office door. 'Sean, do you have a minute?' she asked politely.

'Of course, Sarah,' I responded. 'Please come in and sit down.'

'What can I do to help you?' I asked.

'I've remembered who gave me that glass of wine for you at the wine tasting evening.'

'Are you absolutely sure?'

'Absolutely.'

We could hear some staff members talking as they walked towards my office.

'Shhh!' I said. 'I don't want anyone else to hear.'

I grabbed a sheet of paper and a pen and thrust them towards Sarah.

'Write down the name, but don't say it, and don't tell anyone else. This must be our secret for the time being. You may be in danger if anyone else knows you have told me.'

She nodded her understanding, picked up the pen and wrote a name.

I read the name and nodded. Another piece of the puzzle had fallen into place. 'Thank you, Sarah. You have been a big help.' I smiled to reinforce my thanks. 'But remember, Mum's the word,' I cautioned. 'Not a word to anyone. Now off you go. Don't tell anyone you have been talking with me.'

She nodded and quietly slipped out the door.

Thanks a million, Sarah. Your blood's worth bottling, I thought.

* * *

Wednesday morning Angela and I called into the Magill data centre where the electronic backup files were stored. Angela showed the note from David that gave us permission to access the data. Before long we were running the data tapes through a reader and viewing the information on a large screen. Every now and then I would stop the machine and print a page or two from the backups.

By lunchtime we had been through all the tapes for the last twelve months and I had a sheaf of papers showing the transactions I needed.

'Let's grab some lunch before we go back,' I suggested.

'Yes, please,' Angela replied.

We had a tasty lunch at the Tower Hotel, which was now run by a couple of gay guys who had revamped the atmosphere and the menu. The hotel that had been tired just a few months before now had a new lease of life and the food choices were delicious. We chose the Honey Roasted Duck. It was great.

'Have you all the evidence you need now, Sean?' asked Angela.

'Just about. Still a few loose ends to tidy up, but I think we are finally close to solving the mystery. Let's call into the bank and talk with Frank before we return to the winery.'

'Okay. I'll call and make an appointment with his secretary.' She lifted her phone and made the call. 'He can see us now.'

'Good. Let's go.'

We talked with Frank about anomalies in the financial statements and questioned the possibility of hackers getting into the accounts.

'No chance,' said Frank. 'Our security screening is watertight. I would know immediately if a hacker was trying to get access. You must look closer to home for the cause of money disappearing.'

'I think we are close to solving the mystery,' I said, 'but thank you for your time. I just have one more question. Are you able to say whether all regular payroll expenses go to different bank accounts?'

'I don't know, but I can check for you. It will take some time, but I can call you sometime this afternoon. Is that okay?'

'More than okay,' I answered. 'That is service with a capital S.'

'Not a problem,' he replied. 'I look forward to talking to you again at the next Indian banquet.'

We smiled our pleasure at that thought and took our time driving back to the winery. It was a sunny day, and I had my beautiful companion to keep me company. My smile was beginning to reassert itself on my face. For the first time for weeks, I was sensing I was close to wrapping up the theft of money. There were a few loose ends to tie up, but the pieces of information were beginning to fit together like a jigsaw puzzle. Just a few holes needed to be plugged.

Frank called me later in the afternoon. 'I've found out something very unusual. Quite a few of those payroll payments go to the same account at a CBA branch.'

'I thought you might find that. It may breach confidentiality, but are you able to give me details of that account?'

'I shouldn't really, but this is a special case.'

He dictated a branch name and the account number.

'Thank you very much, Frank. You've confirmed my suspicions. We are now close to solving this mystery.'

* * *

Thursday morning, I checked Tony's list of workers and visitors to the winemaking area. He had been meticulous in his reporting. I checked against my list of people being paid to work in the winery area. As I thought, many more people were being paid than worked in that area.

Then I looked through his list of the visitors to the winemaking area. I thanked him silently for his attention to detail. The list of people from other areas who visited his area, the people they visited, and the frequency of those visits was very revealing.

It was time to have another talk with Marcello. I called him and had a long and detailed conversation ending with several questions I wanted his team to check.

After that I spoke with David. I sketched out my conclusions with him and asked for his feedback.

'Congratulations. I think you have solved the mystery,' he said in conclusion. 'Let's now talk about the reporting session tomorrow. What help from me do you need in bringing this insanity to a close?'

We discussed the meeting format then I returned to my office to call Ken and prepare him for the meeting. Then I prepared some PowerPoint slides for the next morning.

'Have you got the shooter to talk yet?' I asked.

'He says he won't grass on his mates, but I've got a team working on him. I think he'll open up soon. We'll play the attempted murder charge for all its worth.'

Chapter 13

Friday morning, I waited for the senior staff and Board members to arrive in the Boardroom for my final audit report. Ken stood to one side and the two police officers stood near the doorway.

David bustled in, a pile of papers under his arm. Those who had arrived early sat quietly.

Barely suppressed tension floated in the air. Electronic energy zinged from wall to wall. Latecomers tiptoed through the doorway hesitantly trying to appear as inconspicuous as possible. Annoyed faces stared at them accusingly.

Some stared at the PowerPoint screen high on the wall daring it to reveal its message. At this point it merely announced, 'Auditor's Report'.

'All ready?' David asked quietly.

'Ready as I'll ever be,' I responded.

Angela stood to one side ticking names on her sheet as people arrived.

'Only two more to come,' she said quietly.

'Who's missing?' asked David.

'Karl Amos and Stephen Douglas.'

'We'll give them two more minutes and then begin,' said David decisively. 'If they don't arrive, make a note for me to talk to them on Monday.'

My phone rang insistently. I cursed when I remembered I hadn't turned it to silent. Then I looked at the screen. It was Marcello.

'I have to take this,' I said to David.

I turned and put the phone to my ear. 'Marcello?'

'*Amico mio*, I have very important news for you.'

'I'm listening.'

I grabbed a notebook and pen and made hurried notes as Marcello spoke.

'Thank you, Mate,' I said when he had finished. 'I owe you. I have a meeting to run. Talk soon.'

I tore the page from my notebook.

'Show Ken,' I whispered to Angela

She nodded and walked to stand beside Ken. I saw her showing him my note. He lifted his phone and made a quiet call. After that he looked at me, lifted his thumb and gave me a quiet smile.

David moved to the podium.

'Welcome everyone,' he began. 'You are all aware that Sean O'Connor has been conducting an audit of our winery over the last few weeks. This meeting provides the opportunity for you to hear the essential points from his report. I'll now hand over to Sean. Please welcome him.'

A desultory half-hearted clapping gave me my cue to approach the podium.

'I am well aware that audits are not the most popular events in your lives but unfortunately they are necessary in the modern business world. But they don't have to focus only on the problems.'

'There are many good things I have found in this winery, as you will see from these next slides.'

My first slide that showed recent awards won at a number of wine shows.

'In particular, I compliment the winemaking team who continue to produce an excellent range of product under the leadership of Tony Antenucci. They deserve a round of applause.'

Eyes swivelled from the screen to me, to David and eventually to Tony. They weren't expecting to applaud during an audit report. I raised my hands and began clapping and eventually most of the audience joined in. Tony smiled and gave a cheery wave around the room. He gave me a big wink. He was obviously enjoying this unusual event.

'Next I want to compliment the marketing team. They are a cohesive team under the leadership of John Cartwright, and they are achieving well above their weight. This second slide shows a graph of their rising sales figures over the last six months.'

I raised my hands to lead the group in clapping this team. This time the response followed more quickly. *Good. They are getting into it finally*, I thought. I relaxed just a tad.

'Another team that deserves a round of applause is the Secretarial team under Nancy Moore.'

Quizzical looks greeted this announcement.

'These are the unsung heroes of any organisation. They keep the wheels greased, by getting on with what many regard as a thankless task. This team not only does the day-to-day secretarial work splendidly. They do it with good will and go the extra mile to calm an angry customer or win the goodwill of hesitant clients. Nothing is too much trouble for them. They keep the ship on an even keel.'

Nancy's smile was so wide it threatened to burst.

'So, the basics are in good shape. The wine is superb, the marketing is pushing sales through the roof and the organisation is operating smoothly with commitment and outstanding effort from most.

'Sadly, there are some negatives. Quite a few cases of wine have been disappearing. But the person responsible is no longer with us and steps have been implemented to prevent that happening in the future.

Quiet nods from most demonstrated they were aware of the thefts by the circus performer, Damian Delonga.

'A more serious problem has been uncovered. Large sums of money have been stolen from the company accounts. Mr Douglas, who is not here this morning, should have been the first to spot this problem and nip it in the bud.'

A gasp echoed around the room.

'I am not saying that he is part of the guilty team, but his attention to detail was lacking and did not match the commitment I have seen in other parts of the business.

'I have discovered that the theft was carried out by a team of four, one of whom is in this room.'

Heads swivelled; eyebrows raised in question. Just one head, I noticed, stared straight ahead.

'One of those gang members is now dead.'

News of the body in the wine vat had spread through the company like wildfire.

'One is heading for the airport as we speak with large satchels full of cash and one is driving as fast as he can towards the state of Victoria. Both will be apprehended very soon by the police thanks to speedy action taken by Detective Inspector Ken Harris.'

I nodded in his direction. He kept his face straight as if this was an everyday occurrence.

'Now I will tell you a story of avarice,' I began melodramatically. 'There were once two lovers who worked for a large successful winery, but they wanted their own winery. They conspired to steal money from this big winery to fund their new one. Their plan was very simple. They kept adding spurious workers to the payroll and pocketing the salaries. No one noticed. But the Managing Director became concerned with the drop in profits and notified his Board, as is the correct procedure. They hired me to find the cause.'

I looked around the room. I had every eye, every ear. It was a powerful moment, but it was time to draw it to a close.

'The person in this room who engineered the deception and several attempts on my life to prevent me from discovering the truth was none other than the HR Manager, Marie Young.'

She leapt to her feet. 'This is preposterous. You have no proof.'

'On the contrary, dear lady,' I said slowly and definitely. 'Every false entry in the database was made from your computer at a time when you were in your office. The date stamps and IP addresses in the database tell the whole story.'

'You can't believe him,' she shouted to the room, 'he's making this all up.'

'Then tell me why your lover, Karl Amos, is at this moment racing to the airport with cases containing hundreds of thousands of dollars and Steve Lucas is racing to the Victorian border as fast as he can go? Both will be arrested very soon.'

She slumped.

The background noise in the room fell decibels to unearthly silence, punctuated only by audible gasps.

'Arrest her,' Ken ordered decisively.

The police officers moved quickly to where Marie stood and locked her wrists in handcuffs. She was quickly escorted from the room. She gave me a quick glance as she left. If looks could kill, I would be lying on the floor expelling my last breath.

One brave soul started a slow handclap. He was joined by a second, then a third. Slowly the whole room joined in. The slow handclap accelerated to a powerful release of tension and hope for the future.

David hurried over and shook my hand with both his strong hands in a double handclasp.

'I can never thank you enough,' he said emotionally. 'I will always be indebted to you.'

Angela followed and I pulled her into a welcome hug.

'Well done, Big Boy,' she whispered, a wide grin spreading from ear to ear.

Ken walked over and shook hands with David, then Angela and lastly with me.

'You've pulled it off,' he complimented. 'The gunman has confessed she hired him, so you were spot on. I still want to know some of your information sources, but for the moment, well done, Mate.'

I have pulled this one off successfully, but will I be able to do this well in my next challenge? I wondered.

My tiger purred. 'Of course, we will,' he seemed to say.